DO YOU REALLY KNOW YOUR MAN?

A James Hickman Book

Thanks for the support, Nicole
One Love, God Bless you.

Thank you

Jam Hickey

9-29-2006

Copyright © September 2006 by James Hickman

ISBN#: 1-59975-948-9 or 978-1-59975-948-7
Library of Congress control number: 2006905768

Cover design by: www.MarionDesigns.com
Back photo by: Dennis Byron Photography

Printed in the United States of America

Published by
Bullet Entertainment Group
5441 Riverdale Rd. Suite 129
College Park, Ga 30349
www.Bentpublishing.com
Email: bulletent4000@yahoo.com

To order additional copies wholesale, please contact James Hickman at 404-246-6496 or bulletent4000@yahoo.com

DO YOU REALLY KNOW YOUR MAN?

Coming soon to a store near you!

Games Men Play
Love Triangle
Between Two Sisters
Wolf In Sheep's Clothing
When A Woman's Fed Up (Part Two of Do You Really
Know Your Man)

ACKNOWLEDGEMENTS

First of all, I give thanks to God for having a son like Jesus and watching over me all the way, and for being there for me, when I was down in out. Thank you, Lord!

I also give thanks to my Mom, Mary Stewart; my children Decarol, Jamarco, Frankie, James; and my brothers, Anthony, Ira, Tracy and Grady.

PART ONE

Discoveries

SAKINA OWENS

Sakina Owens-Montgomery was sure her marriage to Wallace Montgomery was just about over. She knew it to be so because she had driven him away.

Sakina, a tall and sexy sister with a body and smile to catch any man's attention, had a problem with communication. When something bothered her, she became bitterly quiet instead of speaking her mind. And she held grudges against those she thought had wronged her.

Wallace, the man she married, was a tall chocolate brother who was smart, handsome and hard working. He was an affectionate lover and an old fashioned type of provider. He was also very needy and wanted lots of tenderness in return. Giving affection was not one of Sakina's best characteristics.

She'd try; she'd kiss him back, hold his hand and give hugs freely, but it just wasn't natural for her.

Then they lost a baby. A miscarriage early in the pregnancy that had left Sakina very depressed. And while she very much wanted to be just left alone to cry it out-she had told her mother to stay up in New Jersey-Wallace wanted to pamper her. That didn't work out well. His fawning, whispering, offers of light walks, roses, cards and extreme love made Sakina claustrophobic.

She cursed him out and asked to sleep alone for awhile.

Now, she was over the hurt, back from depression, wanting to get on with her married life and she now could see she had driven her man into the arms of another woman.

Sakina thought she was about to be left because her husband had changed. He was different to her. No longer was he warm and loving. The simple fact was, she knew her husband had found someone else to give his love to.

For nearly a year she waited for it to end; waited for her husband of four long years to just drop her like a bad habit. But instead he just went about his life as if nothing had changed. He left for work, came home, all to the same schedule as he always had. But on the weekends he was ghost.

She cornered him into a vicious argument one Sunday night. He returned her accusations with calm, cool reason; he had answers for everything. He was working late, and he told her he was sorry. He still loved her, and wanted her, but he was worn out. On the weekends he just needed to be with the fellas, to get out and unwind. And he added, "I thought you spent the weekends with your friends." It led to no concrete answers, no he was too good for that. He was excellent at letting her be the crazy one, usually he'd let her rant like a lunatic while he was cool. That Sunday though, he threw curse words at her like never before. And he said he didn't give a fuck what she thought or did.

And that was when she decided to follow him. Whether he was leaving her or not, she just had to know what the fuck was going on.

It didn't take long to discover the truthWallace wasn't hiding his roll.

On a sunny Friday afternoon Sakina rented a car and sat outside the *Bank of America* on Lands Drive in midtown, watching the doors. The bank closed at six on Fridays but her man got off at three; he was a loan officer and had it like that.

There he was, not yet three, but he was off early. He walked briskly to his Mercedes-Benz sports model and took the time to drop the top. He got in and damn, she noticed, he was smiling as he started the car up and moved out.

She tried to be calm, she had no music on, just driving to the sound of her heart thumping in her chest.

He maneuvered onto I-75/85 and then took I-20 out east. *The bitch lives in Dekalb County?* Wallace was speeding. He never sped home from work, she fumed. He hit the far left lane and zoomed out. It was early, before rush hour, but there was a cluster of cars heading the same way. She got into the lane next to his and followed him without a problem.

He got off at Wesley Chapel's crowded exit and moved out across the highway. He turned right on Hairston and stepped on the gas. She got the feeling she knew where he was going. Still, she didn't relax.

He turned into the Tree Forest apartments like she thought he would. This was where her husband's best friend, Robert Flower, lived, she thought aloud. *Oh, he is just hanging at his boy's house getting away from me.* But then she thought this might just be a meeting point, or maybe the home wrecker lived there too.

She turned in nearly a minute after him and saw his car up ahead. He pulled into the lot of Rob's place and parked next to Rob's Cherokee.

She sighed and shook her head. Instead of

following him in she parked at the poolside, backwards, so she could see him walk in. He left behind his briefcase and took out keys. *He has his own set of keys? Shit, they are fucking whores up in there like that?*

She was not maintaining her cool. Most often Wallace talked about he and Rob's relationship as having grown apart. No way had he indicated that he would see the dude so much that he would need keys to the man's place.

Crazy scenarios rolled through her mind. Maybe it was Rob's sister...did he have a sister?...Maybe Wallace and Rob were screwing the same girl...Maybe Rob lets Wallace bang his chick there to save money, men are like that.

She watched her husband disappear into the building. Then she decided to wait an hour, to see for her self the women they were fucking. She'd wait a half an hour after the whores arrive, she told herself, then she would go up to the door and bang her fists on it until one of the assholes in there opened up and they she'd just start kicking ass and she'd demand some answers.

During that hour, though, her mind began playing tricks on her, laying out a whole scenario of how, why and what she had done to lose her man.

It was their baby; the loss of their baby, the loss

of the beginning of their extended family, a crushing blow that had left Sakina on the brink of insanity and suicide. She was 13 weeks pregnant and so gung ho about giving birth for the first time. But then something went horribly wrong, just one of those things, the doctor said, assuring them they could have more. But the depression, and the guilt, took away Sakina's sex drive and love for life. She thought about how she hadn't really paid him much attention after she lost the baby.

He was a good lover, a good man, communicative, lively and affectionate. So why the fuck hadn't he been patient?

Her husband had decided, she believed, that is was better to work late than deal with the grieving. He seemed happier now that he was busier at work.

A little bit of interest goes a long way, she recalled hearing somewhere.

And now, just to make matters worse, she was horny for her man. She wanted him to touch her the way that he did, so gentle, his hands touching, caressing, his full-sized wet lips guiding his heavenly tongue up and down her belly, the damn teasing in her pubic hairs, around her breasts. Shit. All this before he'd get up in her and hit it high and hard.

A week ago she thought she'd never want to see a man naked again, let alone have sex. But now her nipples ached at touch and seemingly she'd get moist down there if the wind blew. She had to have it. It was like she was 14 again, aching to be fucked, and she was married so why the wait?

Her theory now was that he was making her wait because she had acted like she didn't want any. And he was seeking attention from someone else, with the help of his boy. They were probably banging girls, switching after climaxing, and every damn weekend right here. How could she get his attention back? The questions, the finality in the situation, caused her to cry.

"Fuck that!" she cursed and pounded the steering wheel. "Fuck him."

She shook her head and thought it all through yet again. Her conclusion, the answer that she had seen but ignored, was that she had pushed him into the arms of another women and she was going to beat the shit out of the both of them...and anybody else in the apartment.

The thought, kicking ass and the insanity of it all, made her laugh. Then she sighed away the hurt.

Sakina felt justified suddenly for all the devious things she had perpetrated on his personal life...cut into his email...checked his cell phone account online and called all the numbers to investigate who he had been talking to, what female did he now know.

Mean, hurtful thoughts entered into her mind. Running up to Robert's apartment and fighting everyone in there, cursing out her husband for not being a consoling, loving man, or speeding off right then and buying a gun from a pawn shop and killing his lousy, cheating ass...and then herself. Instead of running up there fighting her husband and the whore he chose to comfort him as she had set out to do that night, Sakina found herself fighting off insanity.

Now she was thinking this was stupid. She wished he'd talk to her. Instead of following him around, she should find a way to communicate with him. All this was going through her mind as she sat there, outside her man's best friend's crib. All those thoughts were right, still she felt a need for answers that night, to see for herself, where had he been going and who had he been spending time with.

Sakina left the stakeout just before the crack of dawn, and before she could lose her mind. She had gone home and made herself a big breakfast of three scrambled eggs, two pancakes, a couple of strips of bacon and grits. She cooked and ate to the soundtrack of her life at the moment, Mary J. Blige's sad, soulful lyrics. She had put in all the early albums, before Mary decided to be happy with her life.

The whole evening had rapidly become a nightmare of frustrated desire. Her suspicions of

Wallace had filled her with resentment. She had always been the loveliest girl in her circle; the queen of a debutante ball. She was used to attentive treatment ever since she'd been old enough to walk, and now her husband had gradually grown disenchanted with her as a woman and had started treating her in a totally unfamiliar way.

She had known only the self-assurance of always being the center of attraction, and his worsening degree of sexual distance filled her with fears she had never experienced before.

All of this because of postpartum depression? Bullshit. He had to have been screwing this chick before, was her thought. Fuck him for not understanding and being there when she was ready for his love.

Wallace actually went home later that day. He didn't speak and she didn't either. She walked into their bedroom and the tears started.

They went on about their lives for another week, living in their non-existent relationship.

Then the next week he said to her, "Can you take me to the airport, please?" as if it hurt to speak with her face to face. She broke down and cried right then.

"Why do you hate me?"

"I don't."

"Well, then, I need you and you haven't been there."

"You do? Doesn't, didn't seem that way to me at all."

Wallace said he didn't feel like talking and his sharp, short answers pushed away her desire to have it out. It'll wait, she thought, until he got back. She planned to have it all mapped out in her head, everything she wanted to say, and a strong apology, maybe even a candlelight dinner and the cleavage dress he liked so much.

He had a business trip, he said. And although he hadn't had many of those since 9/11 she didn't question it. They weren't on speaking terms, so what the hell? He's going out of town instead of an orgy across town.

The twenty-seven minute ride to the Hartsfield/ Jackson was all about Mary J. and her 'be happy' newer shit. Neither spoke a word, tapped a finger with the slick beats or hummed alone with Mary's repetitive choruses.

Not even seven hours after she dropped him off she got a call on her cell from a friend she hadn't heard from in awhile. Ayanna Little was a college buddy, and they had some shared memories, wild nights. Now Ayanna was a lawyer and a fag hag, hanging out in a high-powered gay men's clique that made her some serious cash.

After hello and how you been Ayanna simply said, "Girl, Wallace is here with another man and he is hollering at my boy."

"Huh? What?"

It was the loud-ass music. And maybe the booze, her friend calling after months, drunk and thinking she sees Wallace.

"Your husband, Wallace. He is here at 708, is what I am saying."

Sakina's heart clinched. 708? She knew of the place. It was the gay version of Visions and one of Atlanta's hottest nightspots. "You silly and you tripping," she replied sternly. "Wallace is out of town."

"Oh really? So, you two are still together?"

"Ah, yes. And that is not him you are seeing."

"Hold on..." the music and the chattered picked up. Sakina was being carried through the party people. "Wallace, right? Hey."

"Hi." It was Wallace's voice, clear and precise as always.

"You looking good."

"Thanks."

"Having a good time?"

"You writing a class report or something?"

"Just asking, damn. You the one up in here

speaking to my boy and not even acknowledging you know a sister. What, you liking men now? You done dumped my friend?"

"Break out, okay? I am here to have fun not be interrogated."

"Oh yeah. Right, right. Have your fun. Bastard."

"Whatever," was Wallace's reply.

Sakina's heart sank into her belly. She could see the entire scene as if she was off to the side, at the bar and they were across the dance floor. She could see Wallace cut his eyes at Ayanna in the snobby way he can when disturbed.

*The faggotity way he cut his eyes...*she sadly thought...*my husband is a homo.*

Her friend put the phone back to her face, "He mad because he busted. You hear that? That lousy motherfucker.

Sakina's throat clogged. She could not speak. She sat the phone down at her thigh on the bed. She had to hang up but couldn't. She had to go, get away from reality.

On the real though, right then, she wanted to just die and let the hurt, the confusion, the fucked up feelings all be over.

On the day her husband left her he said, "I still think you're beautiful."

DIA STARKS

It was a strange act of Dia's man, Marcus, to take her with him to his buddy's house for a party. It was out of character, it made no sense.

Marcus was a thug. When he went out with his boys he didn't want to be bothered. They did shit with females, Dia was sure, but his dirt never came home. She liked not knowing, she liked that he was cool at home and never disrespectful. As long as it wasn't flaunted in her face, Dia was into man-sharing.

She had witnessed two older sisters have short-term marriages. Both got cheated on, one found her man in their bed with one of *her* co-workers.

Dia understood men just couldn't keep their dicks in their pants. It was too hard, meaning difficult. Especially in a city like Atlanta where the women outnumber the men ridiculously and half the men in

Atlanta are either gay or married. So many single and lonely women and not enough dicks to go around. And many of those women are desperate for the warmth of a man. They'll do whatever, Dia knew.

The women that handle man sharing best have an attitude similar to Dia's. They get from a man what is possible for a particular period of time, and worry little about his arrangements with other women. She understood life had no guarantees, and that life is what you make it.

And so she was cool with the fact that Marcus might have some honeys on the side. At least he supplies a steady income, and that, to Dia, was more important than a faithful man...as long as no female called the house, blew up his cell phone or disturbed their groove in any way. And he had to come home every night. No matter the time, she said, just be home when she woke was her rule.

Dia had no true clue about what kind of man she was dealing with. She had never seen him out with his friends. All she cared about was that she had a man. And the fact that her female friends didn't like him was no big deal in her eyes. That happens, she thought. There were many guys her friends or relatives dated that she didn't care for. Not everyone gets along, was her thinking.

Dia had no plans of marrying Marcus. He was a

great lay, generous with his cash and cool to be around, but he was a dog and the man she would marry would have to at least hide his indiscretions.

Being into man-sharing didn't mean she was easy about their relationship. No, she just didn't want to be lonely.

Dia was a beautiful, strong woman. She was small, thin, dark with large eyes, and she wore delicate outfits. She was a bit shy, her friends thought she was unable to assert herself, and, she was convinced that she was, easily overlooked. She was cool with disappearing when out with her friends, living vicariously through them, which was why she loved hanging with the vibrant bunch of females she called friends.

Dia, despite those inviting eyes, had gone three years in her early twenties without the touch of a man, and the aching and the yearning for male attention was maddening. She tried her church, clubs, on-line dating, and even hookups from friends to find a man and all she experienced was liars and losers.

When she met Marcus she liked him right off. He came on strong and did what he had to do to make her his girl. They had sex the second time she saw him and he moved in with her after two weeks.

Marcus asking her to join him at his boy's crib could have been about respect, she considered.

Dia had bothered Marcus about the fact that she was never invited to hang out with his friends. He would just leave at night and come back in the morning. At first she feared what was going on at these house parties, especially since so many unsavory women hung out with his boys.

He tried to assure her by saying they just hung out and got high. But she knew what weed did to her. So how could he be smoking with other women and not want to fuck them?

What he'd tell her was his solution for being horny was to bring those thoughts home to her, was his reply.

The night she found out just how foul her man could be, he called her soon after she got home from work. She was a school teacher by day, occasional model after-hours. That day, a humid afternoon, she was working a private school's summer session. She came home, poured some cold sweet tea over a gang of ice in a big glass. She was chillin' when he came dragging home. He did a quick change and suddenly he was vibrant.

He came to her and spoke, his voice was alive, unusually clear, but he was subdued. "I'm going to Rod's cribo," Marcus said. "You want to ride?"

The funny thing was there he was finally asking her to join him and she didn't really feel like being bothered. It was that time of the month and she felt cranky, weak and tired. What she wanted was for her man to pamper her, to take her out to dinner, to eat at a nice restaurant, outside among the beautiful people of downtown Atlanta, not with his grimy pothead friends.

But she told him she'd go. Curiosity got the best of her. She wanted to see what they did all night; no way they *just* got high all night. They had to play some cards, Playstation, converse, something.

She just wanted to be reassured. To look in the eyes of the hoochies and see if there was lust in them.

Dia was beautiful. She was tiny, light-skinned with waves of honey-colored hair and great brown eyes. She had been a dress model for Roca Wear for a while. Although she had great beauty, she was approachable and easy to smile.

But around Marcus' friends she felt inadequate. She felt like a lame, like they were all from the 'hood and she was Ivy League.

Rod greeted them at the door, and her man's best friends let his eyes linger as they always did.

"You looking good, baby. I am glad you could make it."

Were they planning for me?

The party began slowly, people joining them and Rod's basement filling with bodies. Drinks were poured; cognac and frosty bottles of Heinekens for the guys. They gave Dia Absolut and orange juice. She took one sip and she was sure she wouldn't take anymore until the ice melted a bit and then she'd ask for more juice.

Marcus had his own bottle of *Courvoisier V.S.O.P* all to himself. He held it by the neck in one hand, his glass with a nice sized shot in the other. They were all drinking and laughing. Then Dia noticed that she was the only one other female at the party. It made her feel funny, guilty for thinking they just get high and screw at these parties. They were just having fun without their females around.

She noticed also that they were all having a jolly ole good time, all of them except Marcus. He just kept looking at Dia as if she had just said the wrong thing, had told his business or something.

He grimaced after a long swig of the brown stuff. Then he spoke. She didn't hear him at first from across the noisy room.

"Stand up," he repeated. "Get up and move over there. The middle of the room."

The chatter died down.

"What?" Dia asked as if he had spoken in French.

"Get in the middle of the fucking room."

She did. Half thinking he was playing, some sort of game was going to begin, and half worried that he was angry about something.

"Now strip," he said. "I said strip."

"What?"

"Bitch don't fuck with me!"

He was angry for sure, and this wasn't a game.

Then she found out what this was all really about. Her man was still upset and jealous about something that had gone down between them damned near a month ago.

At a club a white man had offered to buy her a drink and she told the guy she was with someone. All the man said was "I wish you weren't."

Marcus had peeped the whole scene and was furious. They fought about it and she thought it was over. It wasn't.

Marcus rose up out of his chair in a fury and took her head violently into his hands. "You want to fuck another nigga? I got a trick for you. You fuck going to fuck niggas I know."

His voice echoed through the now silent room. His hand tightened around her throat.

He asked, "Now you love me or what?"

Her tears reached his hands at her throat. She couldn't speak if she wanted to. Her eyes showed she was giving up, as if she was begging for air, to breathe to live. He released her.

"You going to do this. I don't give a fuck. Cry if

you wanna."

She caught her breathe. The silence in the room was hollow in her ears. She rubbed her throat and she softly said, "I need to go to the bathroom first." Her voice and posture hinted at surrender.

"Yo, go 'head, go on and come on back with the swiftness. Do what you gotta do. And then you perform."

She was in the bathroom looking at herself in the mirror, thinking about all the stories she had heard, the legends of the orgies and the torture her man had performed on what she thought to be lesser women. He wasn't like that to her. Maybe they had made him jealous too.

This was insane, she thought, catching the fear in her eyes in the mirror.

She removed and disposed of the sanitary napkin, no spots, good, and came back out and all eyes were lit on her. Her attitude was, like, whatever, and she was going to show him love and respect. She went right up to her man and said, "This is what you want, to degrade me? That is the love you were speaking about? All over what? A man admiring what you got."

"Shut the fuck up," he said evenly. "You ain't talking your way out of it. Get over there and strip."

"You want me to do this I'll do it."

"Shut the fuck up, I said. You doing it. Fuck the tears and shit and the stories. You should have thought on about that before."

You know what, asshole, fuck it. Let your friends see me. See how fucked up a of person you are, was her thoughts.

She had stripped before, and it was no big thing to take her clothes off in front of men. Just like in the club, she knew someone would protect her if things got out of hand, or if a hand touched her.

Dia stepped out of the strappy heeled mules and she shrunk to normal height. She pushed her jeans down her thighs, ever so slowly, wiggling them free. Off came the lace blouse.

All the guys, his homeboys, were alive now. Eyes seemed to feast. Everybody was now looking at the naked girl in the room...even the eyes of the only other female there.

Standing there in her designer panties and lace bra she felt confident that he would put a stop to the game. She knew he couldn't take the probing eyes. She smirked at him, knowing the jealousy was hurting, knowing that he could see she was fine. And she hoped that taught him a lesson. They were only eyes, and she couldn't control them, make them stop looking at her.

And especially Rod's set of grimy eyes. He was

a thug, a thief, a stickup kid, but whenever he looked at Dia he was straight dreamy-eyed, always staring until she gave him the satisfaction of looking him in his eyes so he could make a crude remark. She had never mentioned this to her man, and now she knew he didn't give a fuck. He wouldn't have been upset. This shit that was happening to her right now, it would have happened sooner if she had told, she thought.

Marcus glared right through her. The look in his eyes was not what she expected. They showed no love, no remorse and not a hint of protectiveness.

"Take that shit off," he said. "All of it. Show it."

She did, without thinking. And a hand reached out and took her clothes from her hands. She was naked in a room full of men, and one woman, and that was how her man wanted her. Then her thought was: *whatever he wants. The last thing she ever wanted to be was lonely.*

"God damn," a voice groaned.

"She's lovely, playboy," that was Rod. "Oh yes."

"That's the shit I am talking about," another somebody said. "That's the shit you got at home, for real. Nice."

The brazen scrutiny and comments upset her composure. She sent her arms to cover her dangling breasts. And her feet covered one another.

"Just stand there," her man said.

And she stopped fidgeting.

"Monique," he turned his head to her and she moved to him as if the command was common. "Get on your knees and do like you do."

She dropped down and began opening Marcus's pants. Marcus took a drink and swallowed. He was looking dead at his woman the whole time. And once Monique's wet mouth began working Marcus' shaft, her head bobbing, Marcus spoke to his woman standing there naked.

"See? She don't give me no fucking lip. She don't shine me, she don't clown me. She loves me, all out.

"And she going to finish. Swallow without complaint. Right, bitch?"

Monique nodded yes vigorously in rhythm while sucking him off.

"Get the fucking lights," Marcus said. "Y'all about to do that now."

"Oh yeah," that nigga Rod said.

"Come sit over here," Marcus said, patting the opposite side of the sofa from where Monique was bent blowing him.

She sat. She folded her arms. Her mind was lost.

Marcus said, "Your nipples are hard. I bet you wet." He rubbed her thighs. "Give me some of that tongue. Come on."

Dia hesitated; her eyes were on the female's bobbing head. *This is why he comes here.*

Marcus pushed Monique's head and she stopped with a plop and licked her mouth.

"You gotta party with us," he said to Dia. "This is what I need."

"You need me to fuck your friends?"

"It ain't like that."

"Then what is it like?"

"See, you be running your mouth when I'm needing something, that's what it's about, what it's like."

She sucked her teeth; this was crazy. Her man was high, talking nonsense that led to her fucking his friends. It was depraved, lewd but erotic. With that thought, she considered she must be high too.

"Do this, now. We hanging. Fuck payback. Fuck what you did to me."

She was shaking her head at the insanity of it all when Marcus was up on her, kissing her neck, and he slid his hand slid down her leg to her sexy ankles, that when both were touched the right way made her unstable.

"You thinking about it, right?" he breathed the words into her sensitive neck. "About one guy eating you while two suck your tits?"

Through the dense darkness, as her eyes

adjusted, Dia could see Rod was taking his clothes off, and he was in no hurry, yet moving quickly.

"You got that?" he said to no one in particular. And someone moved and came between Dia and Rod and handed him a tube of ointment that Rod smoothed some over his fingers.

"Bitch, ain't nobody going to be talking to you over and over again. Bend the fuck over."

Her eyes cut to Marcus. He was looking dead at her, still getting a blowjob.

"She don't want to listen, beat her ass," was all Marcus said.

"Fuck is this?" Dia cried. "I prove my love? Is that what this is?"

Rod swiftly picked up his pants and pulled his belt loose with a flitter of noise. He came to her and whipped the belt across her back and then front, quickly before she could move her hands in defense. He gave her four sharp slaps.

"Now do what you was told."

A couple of the dudes were laughing.

Rod said, "Come closer."

He reached out, put one of his ashy hands around one of Dia's thighs, and drew her nearer.

"Oh, no," her mind screamed.

As he pushed her to bend over away from him, her ass cheeks touched his member.

"Come on, hold her."

Someone moved forward to do just that, his cold hands held her arms. The top of Dia's head was inches from his crotch.

Sensing what was in store, she screamed, "No! Not that. Don't. Don't. Please?"

Rod wasn't trying to hear her. No one in the room was. This was what he had been waiting for, a chance to fuck the princess...and he got to do it anally. A bonus. He put a generous amount of the oily stuff on his fingers. Then he spread the cheeks apart until they all saw, or thought they could see through the darkness, an opening. He put a glob of the stuff on his forefinger and thrust it deep in her rectum.

"Tight," Rod said.

"You will be the first, or so she told me she ain't never done it."

"Why you ain't hit it," Rod asked, while getting in place.

"She had me waiting."

"Well, sorry, you get sloppy seconds." Rod spread the cheeks apart again. His solid penis, sliding smoothly on the lubricated skin, readily entered.

Then the pain came. Someone was in her anus. Dia screamed again, in protest, as the narrow passage was stretched, and his balls finally came to rest against the solid flesh.

"Ah," Rod exhaled, "this is the life my niggas."

He looked at the dude holding his victim and said, "Go ahead and get some head, little nigga."

He unzipped and moved her face so as to fit it in her mouth.

"No, no, no," she was saying.

"Suck his dick," it was her man's voice, she was sure.

Dia cried and tried to pull away, the dick in front of her falling from her mouth momentarily, but the boy who was never introduced put himself back in and held her still.

Her man maintained a bitter, humorous laugh while Dia cried hysterically. "You can make it a lot easier on yourself," he encouraged, "if you'll stop fighting it. You're getting fucked either way, whether you like it or not."

Rod said, "She cumming, playboy. She likes it, for sure, my nigga."

Rod drew back and re-entered several times, and he wasn't nice about it. And he was slapping her ass with one hand, her body heaved, quivered with each slap. Dia's choked cry was accompanied by a savage writhing of her hips, but each movement drew the thick cock farther into her spasming tail. Her body shivered.

Then, overwhelmed by the tight friction, he grunted and ejaculated in Dia's ass.

"Yes!" Rod shouted in glee. "That shit was good, my nigga."

Seconds later the guy she was sucking off, who she forgot about somehow, gripped her head and released himself in her mouth.

While the guys left her, sat down and began to light up some weed, Dia collapsed to her knees, crying softly and quivering like a person suffering through a January chill.

"Dia, baby," Rod said after exhaling a cloud from herb. "Now we can be friends. There ain't no friendship between a nigga and a bitch until they fucked. Shit. Fucking is the only social intro that means anything."

His mocking laughter hurt more than the words.

"Fuck you."

"After this? Anytime you want to, my dear. That shit was good."

She shook her head and moved for her clothes.

She looked to the man she had loved for two years. He had a big-tit hoochie sitting in his lap now. She was riding and panting.

"Give me my clothes," Dia quietly said.

"Yeah, get your shit." Marcus said quietly, almost politely. "Go on home, bitch."

That was the shot that made her unstable. Why

would he call her a bitch, because she fucked his friends, because he thought she was a flirt?

The laughter floated by. All she could see, or think about, was the person she had become. A loser intimidated by a man she loved, she thought and the tears finally came. She shook her head. I love him, she thought. She stared at him, him not even looking her way. She loved him and didn't realize it until she was filled with hatred for him.

Dia went on home, crying and in a daze. Marcus didn't come home that night. She called him everyday for nine long days; burning questions and that feared loneliness had her chasing him and leaving desperate questions on his cell.

On the tenth day after the orgy she came home from work and although the layout and furniture all looked normal, she immediately noticed something was different. She looked closer and saw that all her man's shit was gone; his TV, pulled from the electronics in the living room, his DVDs and CDs and even his favorite chair that didn't belong to him. She drifted into the bedroom and the closet was open and some of her clothes had been dropped while he was gathering his gear.

When Marcus finally answered a call from Dia he let her know what she should have been aware of, he was gone out her life.

He told her, "I ain't know you was a slut."

That finally brought the anger out from a woman that was usually reserved. "And I didn't know you were a mean, insanely jealous asshole. I didn't do anything to deserve any of this."

"Whatever. Bye, bitch."

DESTINI MOORE

Destini should have listened to her mother.

Her mom had been divorced twice. What she does now with men would be called sleeping around, and at 51, her mother was pretty good at it. She had no job, yet she didn't want for anything.

"I'll fuck them, I'll party with them, but I ain't waking up with them," was what she said. Her mother told her, "You never know a man until you marry him; still then all you will know about him is that you hate his filthy ass guts."

Men just don't know what the fuck they want, was her mother's theory on why they were idiots, and they listen to each other, so why be with them more than it takes to be satisfied?

Now Destini knew what her mother was talking about.

And she wasn't just dreading having not heeded to her mother's warnings, nor was it because her marriage was on the rocks now. She was more upset because her mother was dead-on right: Men ain't worth more than a good fuck.

Destini had known her man for two years, and had been married to him for seven months. But she didn't know he earned his living robbing drug dealers until one of his vics came knocking.

They were in their large living room, a comfortable section of the large new home they had built out in Lithonia. Boo was on the floor counting money and she was lying on the couch. They were half watching a movie he had rented. His mind was on his money and Destini's thoughts were on the dinner she was preparing; getting up every now and again to check the ziti in the oven.

"I like that dress on you," Boo said about the sundress she used as a lounge-around-the-house-thing.

She smiled. She liked that the fire hadn't gone out of their relationship. He still looked at her with desire. And they still made love every night she could, and some nights they shouldn't have. And she knew why he liked the dress, because it was old, ratty, and it couldn't hold her breasts in place. He'd get a free peak often.

Destini had beautiful, delicate features and very curly jet-black hair cut close to her scalp. She had incredibly thick thighs and hips on normal legs and feet and a mouthful of breasts with those long nipples that men loved to feed off of. She was tall, five-eight, and a slimmy with long legs. Her lips were her money-makers, thick and pouty; they caught a lot of eyes, male and female. Her friends called her Lips, and that was what she had tattooed just below her navel in swooping script letters. She was the innocent looking one through college and always pulled guys no matter how many girls she was with. She was a little silly and loved to eat, a perfect date. Guys didn't have to worry about tossing a serious conversation her way.

Then Boo's cell phone chimed a *50 Cent* tune; which meant that was his boy calling. He didn't say anything until he hung up. It was a short call, and then he said, 'shit, fuck.' He scraped up his money, bolted up and put the money in its spot in a lockbox.

"You have to go out?"

He said, "Yeah, I ain't gonna be long."

Not nearly twenty minutes later after he was gone there was a knock at the door. Destini opened the door without looking first or asking who it was. Danger was the furthest thing from her mind.

There were two big guys standing in the doorway.

The one on her left said, "Sorry, honey," and he

punched Destini dead in the face.

Her knees buckled and the world disappeared. She didn't fall though. Then he punched her again and made sure she was off her feet.

She just lay there in severe pain, her face felt like it was no longer there, like her skull was nub and sore.

Boo saw the guys. He spotted their car coming at him and he made a quick right to get off that street. He drove around and followed them to his house. He saw them walk to the driveway and was happy he had gotten out of there in time. He took what money he could, knowing he had to leave something for them to find or they might get upset and beat the shit out of his woman.

Shit, he thought. He hoped she played cool and didn't run her mouth.

The two thugs tore the house up, looking under and in everything that wasn't nailed down until they found Boo's stash. On their way out the other guy, the one that hadn't hit her, stopped to stand over her. He said, "Damn she fine. Look at them nipples. And them lips. We should collect off of her too."

"No civilians," the puncher said. "Tell Boo he caused you to hurt because he stole from the wrong peoples. If there is a next time it will be all about death for him and whoever we find with him."

The words rattled in her head, mixing with the pain until all she could consider was the threat.

Boo watched them leave; parked and shielded behind the Taylor's bushy driveway. He waited through a couple of songs, until the *T.I.* CD finished and began to replay before he drove less than a block home.

He found his woman on the floor. Her face was swollen and her eyes were glossed over. She had had her hands on her face and she was moaning in pain.

"You okay, baby?"

"They were looking for you."

Her words jumbled out.

"Don't try to talk. Shit, you should have said nothing. You should have just let them take the money, fuck them. What the fuck you say, why they hit you?"

"You knew them?"

"Fuck if I knew them. Let me get you to a hospital. Your jaw might be broke, baby."

She yanked free of his hold. "You knew they were coming. That's why you left. You left me here."

"You taking crazy. I drove right past them. I got a call about something else. You tripping, it's the pain. Just chill."

"Get off me! Just leave me alone. Go! Go back to your hiding place."

DOLORIAN

A month ago Dolorian would have told you that she knew men, that she understood how their little minds worked, that she could control any man with the sway of her shapely hips, or for the wiser fellas she'd hit them with one of her heavenly blowjobs.

Dolorian had been a stripper for four years; she had seen men at their worst, at their weakest and at their strongest. There was no game a man could have played on her. No way.

But damn...

What Dolorian didn't know was how a good man, a man tight with his game and smooth in the handling of his woman's heart could blind and weaken a strong sister into being played like a poker chip.

Dolorian thought she'd finally settled down. She had met the right kind of guy...the kind that had fat pockets and was generous with his cheddar. He had to be a good lover, and somehow had to still have a kind heart after years of being a Black man in America. But Kareem, better known as K-Killa, a hard-core rapper, was not the man she thought he was, and that hurt badly.

After all of them years in the game, no way should she have been fooled. Most of those years up front, up close and personal with thugs, killer, thieves and guys that were plain old bad. She had to learn how to get those kinds of men to spend money on her without ever thinking of hurting her. And most times she got away untouched.

No, K-Killa touched her in a different way, though. He never raised a hand to hit; never even raised his voice when pissed off...Dolorian was the type of woman that pissed niggas off with that fast mouth and vicious tongue of hers. He was mature about relationship shit, showing a caring and understanding of the female ways. He gave Dolorian room to breathe, room to roam, and a man at home she could talk to, take care of and chill with.

She thought that despite his lyrics degrading women and promising to kill lames and his enemies, he was a sensitive fellow, a hard core rapper with a mild mannered demeanor off the stage. She had never witnessed him be violent and most everybody showed him love up in the clubs, on the streets and even behind his back.

What more could a stripper thinking about retiring and having some babies ask for? Dolorian thought she had chosen the right one.

Then a new girl arrived at the strip club Dolorian worked at.

Roxana was a pretty little thing, and right off most of the other girls hated her. She was petite with big ass tits, a shapely *young* body, and an innocent smile...a fucking money maker. On top of those guy-attracting features was the fact that she was exotic, a Colombian girl in an Atlanta Black strip club.

Everybody's eyes, the regular guys, new guys, the other dancers, everybody, watched her, wanted to know her and wanted to fuck her. Even veterans like Dolorian felt a pang of jealousy and arousal. But Dolorian shrugged it off.

Until one morning, at the crack of dawn, the gotta-go hour in the stripping business, K-Killa went to Dolorian and told he is taking the new girl out for breakfast. She thought nothing of it at first, there was an entourage of rappers riding out with him and the new girl...until she noticed no other girls had been invited.

Later that day Dolorian was startled awake by K-Killa quietly sitting on the edge of the bed. "Why don't you lie down?" she asked him. And then, just to be a smart ass, she said, "What, you need a shower first?"

"Fuck you mean by that?" His answer got her fully awake.

She sat up. Through the sunshine and her eyes coming to focus, she could see the red in his blue silk shirt. You could tell it was splatters of blood; and not his.

"What happened?" she asked.

She was sure she was going to hear how one of them stupid asses he hung out with had been shot.

Instead K-Killa hoisted up a Coach travel bag up onto the bed, landed it on Dolorian's legs. She shifted them out of the way and sat up straight.

"This money right here," he said softly. "Twenty stacks. That's you. I gotta be out."

"What? What are you saying? What you telling me?"

That didn't even sound like Dolorian. It sounded like those other females, the ones begging for a man to stay. But she couldn't stop herself.

He looked her dead in the eye for the first time that morning. "I'm married, boo. Straight up. And I am out. That's it."

She was confused. The questions swirled in Dolorian's mind but somehow, even though she had always had a big mouth and never had hesitated to speak it before, she was at a loss for words.

He was shaking his head, taking in her wide-eyed silence. He said, "That honey...the one that came out like that, to the club and shit. She got papers on me. For real."

He stood up off the bed.

"Why you coming at me like this?" she damn near whined. It was the confusion, just like he said; it was also the love she had for him seeping away. "You think you can say this shit and walk the fuck out? Like I won't fucking kill you in here?"

"Yo, save the drama. It was nice, you know that. Ain't nobody was try'na get married right here."

She bolted up.

He turned his back to move for the door.

She went after him and when he turned to face her, his hands up in a pleading stance, she punched him in the side of his head.

The pain shot through her hand. She had planned to box his head, bust his lip, but now her hand hurt like hell.

"You got one. That's it. You raise your hand again and I'ma knock you the fuck out."

"Try it, bitch. And your wife be in mourning."

"That's why I loved you, you got that strength.'

She swung her left hand and was surprised to

connect with the other side of his head. He pushed her off her feet and she sprang back up and tried to engage him in a tussle. He wasn't with it. He pinned her on the bed, fighting her kicking legs and spitting.

"You fight like a girl," he laughed.

"I ain't no joke. You think this is funny?"

He sobered at the sight of her tears. "Naw, never that. I ain't laughing at you, at this, no." Still holding her he said, "I am sorry. I have mad feelings for you. I should have told you I was married, true, but I seriously thought that was done. That I was moving on."

"Asshole."

"Say whatever. I know you mad."

"Dogs get mad. Bitches get even."

He shook his head and waved his hand at her.

"Don't dismiss me," she said.

"You are dismissed. So take them stacks and forget it. You try some shit you just going to get hurt up, on the real."

"Fuck you! You ain't going to do shit."

Dolorian decided to say fuck him and let it go. to count the money and forget the tears for minute. She exhaled while her fingers walked through big head hundreds and sighed, "You never know a man."

He was gone...for a month.

Then K-Killa showed up at the strip club

Dolorian worked in and acted as if everything was cool between them. He gave her a nod of his head and moved through the club.

The sweet, deep and innocent little girl she had hidden inside of her wanted to know, straight up, for real, did he ever love her...did he still?

The tough, street female persona that had crushed over her soft interior didn't give a fuck what he had ever felt for her. She raised her chin to him and gave him a brave nod, silently appreciating and setting to memory all they had shared.

She had found out that his little precious wife and kids lived in Miami, a ocean side mansion. Since he did most of his recording in Atlanta, he was here most of the time and decided to spend it with Dolorian; that didn't make the hurt any easier.

After he and his entourage settled at a table he summoned her over.

"I'm working."

"I'm paying." He fanned a wad of bills.

"All you do is pay," she said as she bent to take her thong down and off her legs.

When she got in motion with a banging *Baby* beat, K-Killa said, "I thought you were going to quit this?"

She pointed to her moist lovebox. "I thought you quit *this*?"

"Never can." He looked at her eyes, which were on his. "Why you wet?"

"My new nigga keeps me like this."

She turned her back and put her ass in his face.

"Bullshit. You ain't seeing nobody."

She gave him a sly smile, "You smart and all that?"

"And you know it. So stop playing."

She shook her head, turned her back to him and gyrated to the beat, letting him get a good look at the ass he used to have nightly. She turned to make sure he was admiring her body, all that used to be available to him and he was.

He grinned, "I can't get one last ride?"

"Ain't you riding your wifey now?"

"You being catty? That ain't fitting your persona."

"Don't act like you know me when you don't."

He motioned for her to come close. She bent, her hands on his shoulders and gave him an ear.

"For real. I am sorry like a motherfucker but I had to go back. Ain't nobody suck dick like you. I miss it."

Unbelievable, was her reaction.

She straightened up, still hanging with Baby's beat, wiggling them money-making breasts. She got back into the dance and let his question fade. When the song ended she reached for her panties and bra and he grabbed her wrist.

"You staying with me tonight," he slipped her three hundred dollar bills.

"That ain't enough."

"But that will get you to sit the fuck down with me though. Won't it?"

They spent the rest of the night talking...not about fucking...and she didn't charge him a dime more. Dolorian knew from experience that not asking for money from a guy like that was the best way to get it. And he no longer was her lover. He was now a mark. K-Killa had her giggling, thinking and conversing about everything else but them in bed.

He wanted some pussy; maybe a last fuck or to be fuck buddies. It wasn't like he straight out asked but the vibe was thick in the air. She was almost cool with any of that, she could see herself taxing this nigga to death, living off of his love of her sexual expertise. But feelings were there. This is the nigga that had her sprung, had her slipping off the game she had learned to master.

So, when the night ended she took him home with her. He followed her red Range Rover in his rimmed up white Yukon. He called her as she reached her place.

"For real, no bullshit right?"

"What you saying?"

"I am saying we cool and we fucking, right?"

"Yes. These questions are fucking up my high and taking away some of my horniness."

"You'll be aroused again," he said. "Believe that. And I got all the high you need."

Two seconds in the house and they were tongue kissing on the couch like teenagers, quiet as it was kept, she loved him for kissing her in the mouth...too many men wouldn't.

Dolorian reached over to him and he felt her hands undoing the snaps on the crotch of his black jeans. His penis jumped out hard and ready and hot into her soft, sensitively massaging hands.

"Hello," she giggled.

"It doesn't get like that for nobody but you."

She nodded, half believing him and half upset that it was no longer hers.

"Come on," he said softly. "Do that."

"She doesn't go down on you?"

Even she couldn't believe she went there.

"Just put your mouth on it. Don't talk shit about nothing else."

Dolorian's grin widened. She rose off her knees and moved to her nightstand.

"What you doing? Where you going?"

"We have to wrap it."

"Come on now?"

She came back with four condoms.

He grinned.

"You better be able to fill all four, tonight."

Slowly and tantalizingly, she lowered herself down until the moist lips of her opening parted sweetly over the head of his penis.

Mmmm, she was so soft and nice inside, so warm and smooth and pillowy.

His hands were like clamps on her soft thighs, as he pumped from beneath her, shoving it in each time at a slightly different angle. She swarmed above him. Her eyes closed almost fainting, unable to do anything but scream at each piercing, rapid thrust.

His hands roamed all over the full brown cheeks of her ass and he gripped the honey flesh, holding her down on his driving cock.

Dolorian screamed out. God, was she loving riding on his dick.

"Shit yeah," K-Killa said. "Take it all."

He pumped gently upward, feeling her tightness swallow more and more of him as she sighed dreamingly and screwed downward with a squeezing motion. She was driving him crazy, and she knew it, frying his brain with the unbelievably intense super reality of her sensuality, the way she threw herself totally into her erotic joy.

She caused the man to grunt. She smiled, and he said,

"This that shit you do."

She was a champ, a winner, with the delight on her face, her tauntingly beautiful, swollen tits, and the way her soft moist pussy sucked on his half-buried dick. It was all nice, so sweet and exciting. Good like this every fucking time and he had fucked up and gave that up for a housewife that couldn't suck his dick right, let alone fuck the freaky way he enjoyed.

Her sweating breasts seemed to grow even firmer, even hotter with his sucking, licking mouth...the clinging walls of her hot vagina tortured his penis until he had to shoot,. Before he knew it, he felt his penis exploding like a roman candle into her body.

Dolorian fought to catch her breath. "That was good, asshole. Now go run tell that to your wife."

PART TWO

Recoveries

CHAPTER 1

Dolorian knew something was up when she checked her caller ID and saw a name from her past. And as soon as she heard her long-time ago hangout partner's voice, she knew the something up was bad.

"Dee, you busy?" Sakina said into her cell phone. She tried to make her voice sound steady but it cracked with the remnants of a bad case of the sobs.

"No," Dolorian said. "I am just chillin'."

"I just need someone to talk to."

"Well listen," Dolorian began, "I am a little busy right now but I don't have to work tonight. Come hang out. Me and a couple of friends are going out to eat tonight. Just come hang, you don't have to talk if you not feeling it."

"I don't know."

"You don't know what? You just want to hang one on one?"

Sakina sighed.

"You could probably use a ladies' night out," Dolorian said. "Am I right? So, come chill with us."

She could imagine, almost see, Sakina thinking it over so she added, "My friends are cool. This will be no bitchfest. Just much love and fun and hanging out."

"Okay. You right. I, maybe, you know, I just need to get out."

"Good. That's what I am talking about. Meet us at Justin's at nine."

Dolorian hated to witness another woman cry, especially hear one sniffle over the phone. The sound and sight would drive her crazy because nine times out of ten it was because of something a man had done, something a strong sister had slipped and allowed a man to cause her feelings to be crushed to the point of tears. And she hated men more than crying females.

Dolorian had very many people, male and female, who she could truly call friends. Most of those relationships had grown out of her job as a dancer. She was very easy to get along with, as long as there were no games being played. Dolorian loved her friends; especially Sakina. They were all she had in

Atlanta. All her blood family was back in Alabama, not missing Dolorian. Often times her friends didn't act like they loved her and she was cool with that.

She understood. Some chicks just didn't understand a stripper. She didn't look at it as hate. Some chicks just didn't understand that all dancers were nasty prostitutes. Some even had brains and treat their jobs like careers.

But when her friends needed advice about sex, how to please their man, or if their man was acting like a fool, they would go to her.

Sakina was one of those friends that came in and out of Dolorian's life. She knew her by her real name, Denise Mincy, the name she went by before she became a stripper in the ATL. They had gone to college together, became roommates during their junior year and traveled to Florida for spring break together. They had a history.

As friends, Dolorian and Sakina were a perfect match, both being opposites. Sakina was the slim quiet one, the bookworm type. She was thoughtful and sensitive.

Dolorian was abrupt, straight forward and tactless in her approach whereas Sakina was quiet. Many people, male and female, took to Dolorian because she was real with hers, you knew where you stood in her eyes and you went from there, good or bad. She was the one that got them invites to the best parties, on and off campus, and would get them dates with cute, money-making boys.

When the two women went out together, Sakina deliberately played the background and followed the lead of the dramatic Dolorian. When they were alone, though, Sakina tended to take the lead. In their room Sakina was the neat, chill one, the one that made sure that when they did have some money in the house between them it was spent right. She kept them eating well and often fed their classmates.

What really happened to their friendship was a kiss. Dolorian took her into an embrace when they were seniors on spring break and tongue kissed her while they were drunk off Cisco and some hydro weed.

Dolorian had kissed many girls through college, but Sakina was different. She had known that from the first time she saw her and them long legs of hers striding through campus. She found herself staring into Sakina's soft eyes and she had felt a familiar tingle between her thighs and the matching hunger in her throat. She knew what that was, and she knew exactly what to do about it.

She was glad to hear Dolorian's voice. Lately Sakina has thought a great deal about their ruptured friendship. After school they went their separate ways yet both ended up in Atlanta. The first year or so after school they spoke numerous times a week. Then the calls dwindled to once a week and then only holidays. And they never saw each other.

Sakina had buried herself in her work to fend off the hurt. As a corporate lawyer, she had plenty of paper work to keep her busy. Now, manless, Sakina considered hanging with her girl more often, and now that Dolorian was a stripper, at least their time together would be exciting. Sakina thought, it was time for a different kind of excitement.

CHAPTER 2

Dolorian's BMW truck turned left into Justin's parking stand. She was feeling pretty good. It had been a good week at her job; a computer convention brought good money to the club.

She stepped out of the car in jeans and heels and enough breasts showing from a low halter top to drink free all night in a male gay bar. The little brown boy valet didn't even notice as he snapped the ticket and gave her half.

Dolorian stepped up on the curb and decided to chill a bit and smoke one before she went in. She dug in her tiny beaded purse and took out a fresh pack of *Kools* in the green pack and her mini lighter.

She told herself she didn't need a new relationship, especially not with a man...men were pigs. All she needed to do, she told herself, was just build on the ones she already has with the ladies she invited out tonight.

It was a beautiful night; she was hoping for a beautiful rest of her life with some real friends.

There was a purring up the street, which turned faster with a down-shift. And then there was Dia, driving cautiously in her brand-new Audi ragtop. It was shiny racing red, immaculate, and looked like it had just been driven out of an auto showroom.

She parked at the valet. She laughed and talked into her tiny phone. She eased herself out of that jewel of a car. Dolorian watched her slim legs emerge first, then her bare arms. Dia was rocking a soft blue Bebe dress, her hair was long now, done up impeccably, wavy and soft.

Dolorian smiled; at least one of us ain't here for a funeral. She shook her head, admiring the natural beauty her barely five feet tall friend was. Dia accepted the valet ticket with the delicate wrists of a cat.

To all watching Dia, including her friend Dolorian, it would seem she was happy-go-lucky, over losing her man. But she was talking to her mother, and she had to be up for Moms though. Her mother hated seeing her daughter with a thug, and Dia would be damned in hell before she let her mother have the satisfaction of saying I told you so. It wouldn't have been important to her mother that Dia had done all a praying wife should have done...even without the rings and ceremony. It didn't matter, Dia would admit; her back to being alone was all that mattered.

She was still talking, loudly, when she got in the door.

Dia was a little giddy about the get-together. The girls hadn't been together in damn near 14 months and she was looking forward to drinks and conversations with loved ones.

Dia saw her friend and blushed. Dolorian was all sexy in tight jeans with jeweled seams and a green halter and stilettos.

"I am here now, momma, talk to you later." She put her cell into her Coach bag.

Dolorian matched her sunny smile and they hugged.

"Wow. Nice ride you got there."

"Thanks. My present to myself. Gotta love me."

"Right, right."

The traffic on Peachtree was still thick as Sakina pulled into Justin's at 9:02.

Dolorian was inside, in the foyer, with one of her friends when she spotted Sakina. She said, "damn," and shook her head. She waved and Sakina caught sight of them.

Sakina was a tall, leggy girl with braces through

high school. By her second year in college her body began to bloom and others took notice. She thought she was getting fat but no, Dolorian would tell her, she filled out her frame with just enough cushion.

"What?" The petite Dia Woods asked, darting her head to see if the rest of their party had arrived. She saw only Sakina in the doorway. "I know you not on the prowl. This is a friends' night out."

"Shut up. That is a friend. A long lost one."

She moved cautiously, Dolorian's eyes on them thighs, and they came together into a tight embrace.

Sakina closed her eyes under her shades. The hug felt so good. She said, "Long time."

"Too long, I'm saying," Dolorian slid her hands down Sakina's body and took her hands.

"Yes."

"Wow, you still look the same, fire as hell."

Dolorian introduced the two ladies, "Dia, this was my girl from college." While Dia and Sakina shook hands and smiled Dolorian took in their differences. The obvious was their height, Dia was barely five feet tall, and she had a nicely small and curved frame. Sakina was near six feet tall and slender; her body too had sweet curves and was filled out agreeably.

The hostess approached them and asked if they were ready to sit. Dolorian took the lead, "Yes ,let's sit down. The other two will be here shortly. I need a drink."

Dia nodded. "Me too, for real. I am trying to have a bunch of drinks and I am not trying to stand up here and wait for the chronically late."

Dolorian played the back. She had to check out her friend from behind. And she wasn't disappointed.

Sakina knew she was on display and she kinda liked it. Attention is attention, she was thinking, and being noticed respectfully is a treat she hadn't enjoyed in a while.

They were seated in a half moon booth facing out into the eatery; easily seen where could see all that was happening.

A waiter came over as they sat and introduced himself as Brain. He offered the specials.

"Listen Brian, we are one short, but we are ready to order some drinks."

"I am with that," Sakina said.

Brian took their drink orders and moved away swiftly.

Watching him walk, Dia softly whined, "Are there any men in Atlanta over six feet tall that can walk like a man?"

Dolorian laughed. "They're somewhere around here."

"They in Buckhead hugged up with a fat, ugly white woman."

"For real," Dia frowned. "Too true."

Just then the fourth person in the *Lady's Night Out* group rang Dolorian's cell phone.

The other two listened in as Dolorian got loud. "No, uh uh. Come on. We'll wait. Bring your butt on."

And then she hung up and put her phone away, saying, "What, is it Men Be Tripping month or something?

Dia came alert, "What? What happened?"

"Des's man punched up her in the face and she's embarrassed to be out with us."

Sakina frowned, "Yes. Why would she want to come out to a busy restaurant looking like lump-lump?"

"The same reason we here. To get out of the house and forget all that."

CHAPTER 3

Destini was already in her car. She had made up her mind to get out, go somewhere, and was so happy to get Dolorian's call to go out for dinner. She felt she needed to get away from her life. She needed to see Dolorian, needed to laugh and live, and her stripper friend was never boring.

Before making the call she had driven aimlessly through downtown Atlanta for almost a half an hour, finally pulling her car into the parking lot of a Starbuck's not more than a mile away from Justin's on the same street.

Even in her agitated condition, she felt a certain security as she sat in the lot, but she left the car's motor running. Cars whizzed by as Peachtree Street was getting busy with folks fixing to have a good time on a Friday night.

She took off her designer shades, dropped the visor and opened the lighted mirror. There she was. The bruises were evident. The spectacular blue and black had faded to a pinkish red on her soft doe-brown skin below her eye.

The sun glasses hid it well, she thought.

She damn sure was going on to the restaurant. The alternative was to go home while her mother was still awake. She was tired of her mother's probing eyes and whispering voice of concern; as if she raised her voice poor little Destini would crack.

Destini thanked God that at least she had a friend and someplace to go.

"Fuck it, here I come."

Within ten minutes she swerved to a stop at the valet sign and popped open her door. The sound of Mariah Carey bellowing out a soft, slow jam filled the air. She took a second to test her footing in heels on the pavement before standing tall out of her Capri blue Mercedes coupe.

Destini handed over the keys to the eager boy and accepted a ticket. She looked down at the creamy beige leather as he slid in and instantly a sprinkle of hateful feelings shivered her bones. She had loved that car before she got it, watching others enjoy the lesser versionsshe got the one with all the bells and whistles, 12-disc CD changer, a DVD player with surround sound, Sirrus satellite radio and allbut now, she despised her ride. She hated that her ex-man had used illegal means to buy it, and now that he was gone it would forever be a reminder of him.

Still, she couldn't get herself to part with it.

She swayed her thick hips into Justin's. She was wearing a fly Vera Wang dress and pair of Wang's latest heels to match. She had the bag too and shades all were gifts from the now kicked to the curb sugar daddy.

It was fairly crowded inside, with people of various shades of brown skin milling around the reception area and by the bar.

Dolorian rose out of the booth and hugged Destini. She whispered, "I am glad you came."

"Me too," she replied as they separated. She waved to Dia.

"Hey girl," Dia said. "You look good," and she meant it. She had coveted that same outfit but her checkbook couldn't handle the cost.

Sakina stood and Dolorian introduced her.

Destini waited for her friends to notice her new shoes but their eyes were focused on the dress. She moved in ahead of Dolorian into the booth and settled in.

"Take them glasses off, Superstar." Dia said.

Destini braced herself, she almost didn't move,

and then with an effort said, "You want to see it? Here you go."

"My God," Dia said, her heart breaking at the sight.

"Happy?" she scoffed.

Dolorian shrugged, "It don't look so bad."

"Yeah, now it doesn't. It looked a lot worse. My face was all swelled up. I looked like Holyfield's old ass after he took a clean shot he couldn't block."

"You okay?" Dolorian's voice softened.

"Fine, and thankful to be out of the house. It's a long story that ends with a punch that I thought had killed me."

"Christ," Sakina said too loudly. "I mean, I am sorry, baby."

"I am sorry too."

"You want to talk about it?"

"No. Not ever," she put the sexy shades back on. "It was fucked up and it is damn near forgotten, so let's let it go."

Dia smiled a little sadly.

With that, the ladies took to their menus, the sound of a live band playing softly playing a Sade hit...but none of them could get the thought that such a pretty woman was sporting an eye jammy.

"We done?" Destini sighed. "Let's move on." She shifted in her seat, smiling, and said, "Shit, how long has it been since the three of use got together?"

"Too long," Dia said.

Sakina let the question float by since she only knew Dolorian. She took her drink and sipped.

Destini asked, "What's up with Tammi?"

Dia said, "She was messy."

"For real?"

"Too messy," Dolorian added.

"She got kicked to the curb awhile ago."

Destini took hold of the menu as Brian, their waiter, came to take their orders.

None of the ladies ordered the same meal and they decided to share.

CHAPTER 4

In no way did Dolorian intend for the ladies' night out she had orchestrated to become a meeting of hurt women. She wanted to get her best friends in Atlanta together, maybe start a tradition, a once a month thing. It wasn't supposed to be about testimonials, but that's where it went.

Maybe it was the booze setting in, losing their tongues and bonding them as friends, but not soon after they ordered their appetizers and dinners, Dolorian threw out a question that started it all.

She simply asked, "So, Miss Sakina, how's that fine piece of man you married?"

Sakina was sipping her drink and after a gulp she sat the martini glass down in front of her. She smacked her full lips and said, "Wallace is straight a punk. And no I had nothing to do with it."

She was shocked her statement brought laughter.

When Dolorian finished chuckling she said, "And why in the world would you say that? What he do?"

"What he do? What he ain't do?" Sakina shook her head and sighed.

Destini boldly asked, "What, you saw your husband kissing a dude?" She didn't know Sakina, and she felt a pang of intrusion for asking, but she surely wanted to hear about someone else's misery.

"I wish it was that simple."

"What?" Dolorian offered her the chance to tell it.

"For what seemed like a damn year he had been going out on Fridays and returning Sunday. At first I didn't care. Our house had been a solemn place. I was a bitch, well not a bitch, but I wasn't communicating. I, we I should say, had lost a baby and it hurt me bad."

"Yes, say bitch because shit when was this? You didn't call me or anything? Damn."

"Talking was the last thing I wanted to do. It was just, I mean, depression came and took over. I was shot, pushed off a cliff. I was in bad shape."

"And this nigger decided to dip out?" Destini snickered. "With a dude?"

"Look, at first I really didn't care what was going on. He went out and I was like so what. He did try consoling me in the beginning but I wasn't trying to be consoled. Basically, I was angry because I couldn't believe this had happened to us, and then I wanted to try right away to get pregnant again but he didn't want to. He said maybe this was a sign. And that's when I was like, fuck him."

"He was going out to see some dude?"

"Yeah. I followed him one Friday. And he went to his best friend's place. Nothing happened for hours, or so I thought. I left them alone and he comes home Sunday, doesn't speak and we went on about our lives, living a non-existent relationship as if it was normal."

She paused for a sip of her martini.

A bus boy arrived with their salads and appetizers. Before they could get good into eating, Dia had to know the whole story. She asked, "So, what happened? How did you find out Wallace was gay?"

Sakina had forgotten that she hadn't finished the story. She was feeling good, getting it out had been therapeutic and she shrugged and continued, "The next weekend he reminded me that he had a trip out of town. He asked me to drive him to the airport. Why he feel he had to lie like that? I don't know."

"That's how they do it," Destini added. "Lie to be lying. Scheming on stupid shit."

Dolorian asked, "How did you find out he was lying?'

"The old fashioned way, somebody hipped me to it."

Dolorian smiled.

"A friend of mine, a fag hag, she used to like to hang out with gay men, called me and she said she was at 708, a hot club, the gay version of Visions."

Dolorian nodded.

"And she said that Wallace was there with a man. My heart clinched. But then I told her that Wallace was out of town. She said, 'Oh really? Hold on.' I could hear that she put me on speaker phone and she went up to Wallace. She said. "Hi Wallace." And his voice came through thick and heavy. She held a damn conversation with him."

Sakina's throat clogged as if she was experiencing it brand new again. She took a sip of her water and said, "I had to hang up. I had to go. I had to get away from reality."

"Damn," Dolorian said.

"I mean, I was not going to go out and chase him down," Sakina added, "try to bust him, but I could not sit at home and shit. I went down there and staked out the parking lot like a super cop. I called my girl and she was like, 'He still here, he a little busy though.' Homeboy was on the damn dance floor and shit like two *Brokeback Mountain* fags or some shit."

The ladies laughed, even Dia cracked a smile.

"Yeah for real. And after a while he and his boy, his so called best friend from college and shit, came out. They stopped at Lamont' pickup, his best friend, and the motherfuckers hugged and kissed as if they were going off to war and might not see each other again."

Destini's mouth gaped. "My Lord Child, no. Ill!"

Dolorian laughed.

Dia, her lips snarled in a grimace, shook her head in disgust.

"That's Atlanta for you," Destini said.

"I mean, what do you think happened? You think he was always gay and just was hiding it?"

"I don't know," Sakina shrugged. "Like it matters?"

"Homos are made, not born," Dolorian offered.

"He's gay because that's how he has decided to roll. How about that?"

Dolorian said, "He's gay because men ain't no fucking good."

Destini frowned and said, "Let me ask you something?"

"Yeah?" Sakina replied.

"Was your sex life good or what? I mean, can you tell if your man is a punk by that?"

Sakina sat back, folded her arms and sighed. "Our sex life was fine, I thought," she said softly. "Besides the fact that the nigger wouldn't and couldn't go down on me. That fool doesn't know the joys of eating a woman. But obviously, he likes a dick in his mouth all right."

"Ill, okay?" Destini squirmed. "Mental picture bad."

Dolorian and Dia laughed, more at Destini than their friend's vivid description.

CHAPTER 5

The bus boys brought the food, and the ladies claimed their plates.

"Can you tell our waiter to come over here?" Destini asked. He nodded and was gone. "I need me another drink."

"Me too, for real," Dolorian said.

Brain arrived. "Is everything fine here, ladies?"

"No," Dolorian frowned, "We need another round. And tell them to use the real booze this time. We grown, we can handle it."

Brian laughed. "Yes ma'am."

When he was gone the four women ate in silence with intense appreciation, chewing on each other's thoughts as well as the steaks, chicken and pastas.

Destini downed the last of her *Remy Martin* and took center stage. "Well, listen. Not to keep the whining going, but I need to get something off my chest. Something I just need to talk about. And after I don't need any lectures," she looked to Dolorian. "I just need to get this off my chest to some friendly ears. First of all, Boo caused this, he didn't physically do it."

"That's okay," Dia said.

"No. It's not okay. I had no idea he was that kind of asshole, to get warned and not warn me, not tell me shit and leave me in harm's way."

"What?" Dia asked.

"He got a call first, I know he did, and he left me behind. Maybe the thought they wouldn't do anything to me, but he was so wrong."

"Shit," Dolorian said with a mouthful of pasta, "I had a boyfriend in college who used to shove me around, off my feet sometimes, and I'd cry, he'd say to me, 'Stop being so dramatic. It's not life I beat you up or anything."

"My God," Dia said shaking her head.

Destini took a sip and went on, "I called my momma. She was the only person I could think to call. At that time I still didn't want to get Boo into trouble. She came and took one look at me, called an ambulance and the police came."

The women around her were quiet, but she was warmed by their eyes, their looks of concern. Sakina held herself quiet, with effort. She thought the discussion was a bit off, thought these good-looking women were trapped into dating morons and assholes. And then she considered what else could be out there, now that she was out there, and she became sad.

Destini was saying, "He called me the next day. His first reaction, the first thing he said to me, no how you doing, baby, where you at, none of that. He said, 'You let them take my shit?'"

There again was an intense silence.

Their waiter came with a clear glass pitcher of water and freshened everyone's glasses. When he was gone, everyone looked at the new water as if it danced in their glasses. No one seemed able to speak anymore.

What else was there to say?

Dia enjoyed the quiet. She was raking her fork through the soggy mac and cheese...but that was the distractionthere was not enough cheese.

Her mind was not there and through the prolonged silence she felt no pressure to speak, to answer another rhetorical question or chimed in on how fucked up men can be.

Dia's thoughts were not in Justin's, not at that booth and not truly worrying about how little cheese P. Diddy's baked macaroni had that day. No her mind wasn't even stud'n all or any of that for real. She was back to the morning she realized she didn't know her man like she thought she did.

She messed with the macaroni noodles contemplating what a lie it was, that old wife's tale, that you don't really know a person until you live then. Well, she lived with him how long? Damn near two year and she had no clue he was an absolute jerk.

Her friends seemed to be living a happy life. The grass ain't greener, she had discovered that night.

"What's up with you, Miss Lady?" Dolorian snapped Dia out of her train of thought. "You mighty quiet over there."

"Nothing, I'm cool."

"You sure? You don't look cool. You look like all this is affecting you."

"It is affecting me, shoot," Dia said quietly. "I mean, I thought the fucked up shit my man had done to me made me odd."

"Please. Not even," Dolorian said.

Destini shrugged her shoulders, "Spill it."

Sakina was now the quiet one, looking at Dia, waiting for her story, praying it would not be as serious as hers or Destini's.

"I have a broken heart," Dia began.

"Girl, please, now. Broken hearts belong in Lifetime movies," said Dolorian. "They don't go with the times we live in."

Destini scoffed. "Please. There are more broken hearts than there have ever been *because* of the times we live in. The whole 'there aren't enough men to go around' thing leads to broken hearts. In fact, I'm sure any heart we know is so cracked and split it's just a mess of scar tissue."

Dolorian took in Dia's deep, attractive chuckle. She considered how pleasant she was to look at, but she was not all that smart. Dia always made it seem so drastic to not have a man in her life. She so wanted to ask Dia, how a man could trust a woman who falls in love with him only after they have made love?

Now Dia was ready to tell. More ready than she could have ever imagined. She began, blurting it out at first and then slid right into the story when she had everybody's attention.

"I got my heart broken because I never knew what I was looking for in a guy. I just figured I'd know when I met him. Obviously I was wrong about that because I thought my fiancé was Mr. Right and he was so Mr. Wrong."

Destini shrugged, "What in the name of Christ happened, shit?"

Dolorian took a swig of her martini and grimaced. She said, "I mean, dang, it can't be all that bad."

Dia smiled at Dolorian gratefully and said seriously, "Marcus wanted to teach me a lesson."

The ladies got quiet. Dia felt all eyes come to her.

She sighed, dragging her fork through her food. "My lesson began at Slice."

"Slice?"

"Yeah, this pizza slash bar downtown. Peters Street."

"Where?"

"Across from the big U-haul place."

"Fuck that, go ahead with the story."

"This white dude was eyeing me big time. Marcus moved away to holla at one of his boys and the white dude took his seat. I turned my head. He offered me a drink and I said I was with someone. And that was that. The white dude said 'I wish you weren't' and he went back to his spot. But no, Marcus went off. Made a scene and shit. Trying to fight the dude.

"When we got home he was still furious. 'You want to fuck another nigger?' he said. 'I got a trick for you.'"

Dolorian sucked her teeth. "Asshole."

"For real," Sakina sighed.

"When we made love that night after the fight he had me get in his lap and he made me tell him I love him like a hundred times."

Dolorian had her mouth opened wide in awe. "Oh, look now, this man is a fucking fool."

Again she ignored Dolorian and went on with her story as if she had to, as if it was therapeutic.

She couldn't tell all the details, it got quiet when she spoke and her mind ran through the details, making her feel stupid for what she had gone through.

"Then the next weekend he asked me to join him out with his friends...God, I was so wet. Drunk, I don't know.

Dolorian licked her lips.

"Of course I never loved him." Dia felt so ready to cry. "After he had me fuck his friends..."

"Oh my..." Sakina yelped.

"...Then he told me he loved me but that I was a nasty bitch and he couldn't fuck with me anymore. He was mad at me because he thought I enjoyed it."

"Did you?" Dolorian asked.

She just cut her eyes away from the stripper.

"What?" Dolorian didn't see the bad in it. "I mean, damn, how many times did you cum?"

"It was rape."

Dia lit a cigarette (unusual for her), sucked deeply, and blew the smoke at Sakina's martini.

"There's no smoking in here," Destini pointed out.

"Call a cop."

"But she here telling us about it. She ain't go to the police."

"For what? What they going to do? She was drinking with a room full of men."

"He's an asshole and like you people think it is okay to take advantage of a woman because she gets moist."

"You feel violated? Then get a nigger arrested or shut the fuck up about it."

While her friends debated on what she should/should not have done she thought about the details she had left out of her story. Like how she had always denied her man anal sex. But that night, when he had her vulnerable and being violated, he took it. He hit it hard, pumping his big dick into her tight hole as if he never cared about her, never loved her. All the while telling her to keep dude's dick in her mouth.

And sometimes she could still feel the pain.

He never loved her, she finally considered. All that time she had thought she was bringing out his meanness by not being the women he desired. No, now she could clearly see he was not a good man, not a good man for her.

"I don't know," she said. "I am better to just be done with him and move on. I found out later that whenever I was out of town he had been bringing home white chicks and fucking them in our bed. And paying them too."

"Jesus."

Oh, see, he had white issues. He wanted a white woman and when he saw that white boy giving you attention he freaked."

"What an asshole!"

Again she cringed at that word and then, as quickly, shook it off. "I am just happy I don't have anything."

Sakina cut her a look, and then backed her angry eyes away. The girl don't know, she can't tellcan she?

"See, the problem is y'all. Y'all are your own problem. Y'all not listening to yourselves. Sex, it's all about sex. All the damn stories. I mean, you don't think that maybe had y'all been different none of this would have happened."

"Please, Wallace was a homo. I can't suck a dick like a man."

Dia shook her head defiantly.

Destini was considering it. Then she shook her head. "Whatever."

"You bitches complaining about the wrong thing. You should be complaining that we all are, have been, stupid for men."

"Fuck you," Sakina said.

"Anytime."

Dolorian's laugh eased the females, but they

had been knocked silent as the significance of Dolorian's words sank in.

"Look, I see all this shit."

"Why because you a dyke lesbo?"

"No. Because I deal with men."

"You don't deal with men, you deal with hounds."

"No, I see them all in the club. And there are some good ones. It what we do, how we present ourselves that they react to."

The ladies got quiet. Seemingly surprised by the sense Dolorian was making. And Dolorian took advantage of the attention to take center stage.

"Men are fools."

"And what are we?"

Sakina reminded her of Morris Joe.

Dolorian bristled. Mr. Joe, she sighed angrily. The man had her heart and crushed it without any afterthought.

"You had to go there."

"All the way there."

"That was college. And that proves my point. I have been stupid for a man. Fuck 'em all."

"Didn't you think he was all that. Shit, you did some wild and crazy action before you found out"

"Found out what? He..."

She was shaking her head and folded her arms.

Then the table of women settled in amazement.

Their bold leader was shell shocked.

"Look, I don't have a sad story. I have old ones that I forgot. The last man I had was okay. Normal Nothing specially good or bad. He just wasn't trying to lock me down."

Sakina sat up to announce that she has given up sex, given up men, because she can't be bothered.

The tipsy ladies all laugh.

"I am with you, sister girl," Dia announced.

"But I mean it."

"Well, good for you honey. Welcome to the club."

Sakina sobered.

"Whoa," Destini had been laughing so hard she had fallen down the booth and was nearly under a table. But at the hint that one of them was converting to lesbianism she sat up.

"Fuck this," Dolorian announced.

They all looked to her as she stood above the table, breasts jiggling. She pulled out money and tossed it on the table. Two crisp one hundred dollar bills; much more than her share.

"Let's go. Let's go see some ass. Male ass. Dicks, broad chest, muscular thighs and airheads, all that. It's what men do to forget their troubles, to unwind and shit."

CHAPTER 6

At the valet stand the tipsy women talked a bit too loudly. They filled the cool night air with profanity and laughter.

"You rolling with us, sweetheart?"

Dia cut her eyes. "No thanks."

"For real? You just going to leave mad? Mad at me?"

Dolorian's eyes caught Dia's slim brown fingers twist together and lock. The hands were saying: "Why do you hurt me like this?"

"You simply don't understand," said Dia. Her eyes reddened and filled, and she determinedly blinked them clear.

Dolorian sobered. "What is it? What are you saying? What is it I don't understand?"

Dia just shook her head and when she spotted her car she moved to it. She slid in the driver's seat and the young man closed her in.

Dolorian shook her head, "We just lost one." She looked to the remaining two to find Sakina was damn near in tears.

"What? Not you too?"

"I gotta go home. I mean, it's just..."

"What? We trying to forget here, that's what this night is about. What? You think I was too hard on Little Bit?"

"No, no. It's me. I just need, I just want to be alone for awhile."

"Being alone, no, that's not cool. He's gay, let it go. You gotta live."

"It's more to it. It's...I wish that him leaving was the end of the story." Sakina went on, "I am being straight up. I don't just think I am giving up sex, I know I am. I know I am because I am probably HIV positive."

"Oh no," Dolorian felt like she had been kicked in the stomach.

"The package?" Dolorian looked at her friend wipe the tears, she couldn't figure out what she was saying and then it dawned on her.

"My god."

Sakina broke down.

Destini heard the sobs and instinctively came to Sakina's side.

Dolorian asked, "Wait, did you get tested?"

"No. I got a letter from the health department after he left."

"Fuck that. I'll go with you."

There were another group of attractive brown women waiting for their cars behind Dolorian and her friends and one said, "Hello, move the cars."

"Fuck your car bitch," Dolorian said. "I'll leave my car right here for two days if I want. You wait and shut the fuck up."

Destini grinned. "All righty then."

"No fuck her. Don't be hurrying me. Who the fuck she think she is, Gloria Vanderbilt out this bitch?"

Dolorian's phone played it's cute little tune. She looked to see it was Dia. "Yes. bitch?"

"Where we going?"

"TDH! You know the way, they got your picture up on the wall!

"Come go on out with us? Don't let your night end alone. You can stay with me."

Sakina was shaking her head. She was feeling pressured. She wanted to stay with and more folks had come out to claim their cars.

"Fuck the bullshit," Dolorian said. "No more

tears, okay?"

Sakina made eye contact, and in her soft brown eyes were full evidence of a lost soul.

"I am sorry, baby. So sorry. Hurting you is not at all what I ever want to do."

Sakina nodded. "I know that. I'm just really fucked up in the head right now."

"Listen, we out having a good time, friends, so let's keep this shit going."

Sakina so wanted to get to her bed and cry it all out. She just wanted the next day to come, and with it, she prayed, would come all the answers to her confusion. But she went on to the strip club. And you know what happened? She had a good time. More drinks, more fellowship and plenty of laughs.

Tall Dark and Handsome was a male strip club downtown, maybe ten minutes from Justin's restaurant. They ladies convoyed down Peachtree and turned down a by the old Macy's building to a crowded parking lot. The building housing TDH looked like it could have been a movie theater back in the day. It actually used to be an playhouse, home to productions of small budgeted stage plays.

TDH was now a place where women, and men, lost their minds to drinks and the sight of tight, sweaty, muscular male bodies gyrating and pumping on the tiny stage. There were private dances and other stuff going on there that made the place a hot strip club.

They ladies parked and joined the crowd moving in through the darkened doorway.

Sakina couldn't help but pray she didn't see Wallacedancing or getting a dance.

Dia got picked from the huge throng of horny and drunk females to be a part of Andy Conda's stage show. The honey brown skinned muscle man with the meaty cock inside of an elephant thong.

Afterwards, even after the bouncers had to take Dolorian out by her arms, out in the trashed parking lot, as the moon gave way to an orange sun, the girls were still giggling...all of them except Dia. Her small body let some of that liquor out the way it came in. She puked at the side of Dolorian's Range Rover.

"Girl, no!" Dolorian laughed, "not them tires, please. Them rims cost more than your momma's house."

Dia might have been fucked up but she was strong enough to pop a middle finger at X.

Dolorian was holding Sakina by her arm, their bodies so close. "Girl, ain't you happy you hanged?"

"Ah, yeah."

"Bitch you should be. She laughed so hard when Dia fell off the stage milk came out of her breasts!"

"Bitch you a lie!"

"Bitch, check your bra."

CHAPTER 7

Although she got hour close to three in the morning and tipsy, it was hard to get to sleep that night for Sakina. After tossing and turning for a while, she had given up on falling asleep and got up.

Out of habit, she eased out of the bed as to not disturb Wallace, and she hated herself for it. She went into her kitchen in her short nightgown, opened the refrigerator and poured herself a healthy glass of orange juice and added some Grey Goose to it. She switched off the alarm and walked out to the patio and stretched out on one of the chaise lounges that rarely had a butt in them.

The neighborhood was quiet, kinda scary. She was behind the six-foot high wooden privacy fence Wallace had put up the day they moved in.

She felt the night breeze and watched the dark sky, sipping her drink until she dozed off without realizing it. The sky was beginning to lighten when she woke up. She gathered her glass and went inside with hopes of finding something fulfilling to do with her weekend.

What was there to do on a Saturday single?

Nothing, she thought. It was back to the life of misery for Sakina. It was all she thought she had left.

A sort of flash popped off in her mind of how deaf and stupid she'd been for months and months. Or maybe not stupid. Maybe just too cowardly to admit the hard evidence of all that she'd seen and heard. New shame and new fear came to her then in equal portions.

And she had let him get away with it. She hated herself then, and she hated him. She almost began to weep, but stifled it. Her rage became pity, and then self-pity, because she lacked the spine to bear the burden of the wrong, to face herself,. And because, in the end, she knew that meant she was no better than any of her friends from last night.

Sakina swallowed hard. For weeks she had had fantasies of cursing him out.

"Listen, Wallace. Just listen. I don't want to have anything to do with you."

Wallace so nonchalant. He said he saw this new doctor. 'You need to have AIDS test,' he says like it's no biggie. 'Everybody I have been with in the last couple of years needs to."

Wallace said he was at the club for a serious reason. To find out the real deal. He found out...He found out that his joy for dick got us killed. He had to find out for sure if he had the package."

"Shit."

All she could think to do was call her friend. Dolorian answered on the first ring, and she sounded wide awake.

"I was trying to get more information out of him but he was so damn vague."

"You should have been kicking his ass."

"I was halfway calm because I can't believe this shit. This motherfucker killed me, Dee."

CHAPTER 8

Before Destini went to sleep last night, lying in the dark, her head swooning from the booze and partying, she had made up her mind to never see Boo again. Fuck him, was her thought.

Destini woke with a headache, a slight hangover.

She popped three Advils and started to make breakfast. The doorbell kind of surprised her, who could it be at eight on a Saturday morning?

It was her man. Ex-man.

"What do you want?"

"You."

"There is no me for you, so bye."

He put his foot in the door and pushed his way in. She knew better than to fight him.

"We have nothing to talk about."

"Where did you go last night?"

"Please leave?"

She caught his eyes on her braless breasts. She folded her arms.

He kept moving toward her and she had to send her arms out to keep him at bay. He stopped.

"baby, I love you. How could you think I would have something to do with you being hurt?"

"Please just go?"

"No. I can't just leave," eh slid his hands to her breasts. "This me right here."

She pushed his hands away.

"You had another nigga up in you?"

"no," she was frowning and shaking her head. "Why don't you just go. Go be with your gangster niggas and leave me alone."

He moved in closer, pinning her to the sink's counter. His arms wrapped around her and he moved to kiss her. She turned her head and he had only a soft cheek to kiss. Still, he put tongue on it.

"That dude that did that, he's dead."

"What did you do?"

"Avenge my wifey. That's what."

She was shaking her head again.

His hands was under the T-shirt and he had a full grip of her breasts. She didn't slap his hands away so he continued. He cuddled them in his palms, found her nipples with his fingertips, teased and rolled and plucked. She arched into him with a soft, hungry cry.

"I gotta suck these. God I fucking miss them."

"No, please, I don't want you. Just leave me..."

His head snapped up to meet her eyes. "Don't ever fucking say that again. You love me and that shit shouldn't have gone anywhere."

When she still hadn't physically protested, he pressed his lips to hers and she accepted his kiss.

He took her hand and put it on his penis; he had opened his jeans somehow that quickly.

"See how it fucking misses you? Why you playing me? This is where I belong."

She was frowning now. Her breathing quickened. She made a soft sound.

"Boo?"

"I have missed you so goddamned much," he groaned that sentiment against her lips.

All the anger she'd felt, all his frustrations and worry, had exploded into blinding passion.

He led her out of the kitchen, food cooking on the stove, and into their living room. When he lowered her to the couch, she didn't complain. In fact, she opened her legs to make room for him, allowing him to settle into the cradle of her body.

Boo tugged her shirt off over her head and heard a seam rip. Destini didn't care. Already her nipples were tight, flushed dark. He lowered his head, closed his hot mouth around her and sucked.

With a long moan, Destini shivered under him, trying to wiggle away from him, instinctively fighting such an onslaught of pleasure even as her hips rolled against his, stroking the length of his thick penis, further initcing him.

He pushed up and she knew it was time to get naked. She took off her shorts and readied herself for invasion.

"Come here," he said standing, his penis pointing straight at her.

She knew what was up. She dropped to her knees and took his penis in her mouth, whole, and sucked it hard. She moved back and forth, slowly until he stopped her abruptly.

"That's the shit right there, but I need to be up in you. Feels like years."

He felt her tighten, heard her breath catch sharply. And he pounded away.

"This shit is mine."

She was panting hard, her eyes closed, teeth clenched.

He came closer, his whole length buried deep, grinding her into the couch's cushions.

"You can't leave this dick. Hell naw. You addicted like me."

Her eyes opened and she couldn't protest.

CHAPTER 9

Dia still hated her man and what he had done to her. But she missed him.

She was blowing up his cell phone with the intentions of telling him off but all she wanted was to hear his voice, to hear him say he wanted to see her, that he was coming by.

That didn't happen.

First off, he never accepted any of her calls. So what she had to do was run into him. She went to his job and he ignored her. He went on about his business of tuning up cars, changing oil, whatever, as if she was not there. She went to his momma's house and he ignored her.

When he finally acknowledged her, he snapped. She parked next to his car at a mall in the 'hood and waited. He came out, with Monique

"What the fuck?"

"Why you doing me like this," she sobbed.

Monique continued to the ride.

"Look, get the fucking message, find a new love."

He moved to the driver's side and Dia grabbed at him.

"You nasty, now go on."

"Just talk to me."

"I'm telling you straight, we done."

"No..."

Maurcus shook his head, "You need to stop. Go live your life. Go strip like your girl. You could do some more orgies."

He dropped into his black Cutlass and fired it up.

The car skidded back and then moved away. And, for a second, she felt a deep painful hurt. But then the peace came. Just for a moment it washed over her like cool water on an August afternoon.

CHAPTER 10

Three days later, just an hour or so past the noon of a soft Tuesday, Dolorian cruised her SUV into the lot of the Golden Leggs strip club, her second home.

Dolorian was cool with being single again. Now she had time to flirt and make money with other rappers and R&B stars.

She went to work early, trying to eat the take-out soul food dinner. But she was interrupted in a nice way. She was in the dressing room alone, only a dozen women were working the lunch shift. One of them, Sindy, a thick Spanish honey with long legs and a killer smile, went in on Dolorian.

"Damn, that smells good, mommie."

"You want some?"

"You going to feed it to me?"

Dolorian smiled. That was the sign...they were going to fuck.

Busy with Sindy, she forgot to cut her phone off. Then she heard *The Game* spitting fire, the ring tone she had set for Sakina.

"I gotta take this call."

She heard Sakina sniffling, and then her friend said, "For whatever it's worth, I always loved you."

"'Sakina?"

"Good-bye."

Sakina hung up.

CHAPTER 11

Within a day or two it seemed pretty clear that Sakina was going to be fine.

Dolorian visited her in the hospital for the entire time it took for her to get better. She could not believe that one of her most stable and intelligent friends had tried to commit suicide. Just because your girlfriend acts sophisticated, do not assume that she has the answers to life's tough questions, or that she has it going on.

They had lunch and dinner together. Every night in her room for three days before they spoke about why they were in the hospital until Sakina said, "What I did was pretty fucked up."

"Yes it was. To call me like that and then try to kill yourself."

"It was a call for help. Cowardly."

"I thought I had AIDS," Sakina added softly.

"It's okay."

"I took a whole fucking bottle of pain killers, thinking they were people killers. I just wanted out. Out from it all, away from it all."

"Well, to hell with it. It's done, over. Luckily you ain't no killer. And here I am."

Sakina shared a room with two other patients, and her folwers overwhelemed the tiny room. The second time Dolorian visted, she couldn't take the clasutropbic setting.

"We getting you your own spot to shine," was all she said. "Fuck dying."

The male nurse at the center desk was curt. "And which health plan would you like us to put this on?"

"Cash, Miss."

Once Sakina was settled, afew hours later, Dolorian threw her a party in the new room, with Dia and Destini and take out from the Cheesecake Factory.

"Dee, girl, you are going to get me in so much trouble."

"Fuck male nurse, and fuck dying," she said again. "Bitch, eat."

Sakina's recovery time passed in a haze. All she knew was that the stomach pains at first, then the hunger. And while leaving the hospital with Dolorian at her side she wanted so badly to quench that hunger.

"You know what I got a taste for?"

"What's that?"

The eyes of the male nurse widened.

"I want schrimp pasta and cheese biscuits."

"Why you have to say it like that, clutching the pearls?"

"Because, bitch yes, I am hungry!"

"Niggas love Red Lobster."

"And I am going to get me a lobster tail with it. On the side."

"Sheesh."

"What, and you not a nigga? I done seen you up in there crack crab legs like a faggot angry with his Barbie doll."

"Really, like that? That's how I was doing it?"

"In deed."

"Well, my mind right now is elsewhere."

"What you want?"

They reached the Caddy.

"I'd never thought I'd say this to a woman, but after a month in the hospital, I am hungry..."

"What's that, love?"

"Would you cook for me?"

"Bitch, you getting more than that. My enemies can get a meal. You gonna get service. And with a smile."

"Shit, well alrighty then."

Sakina stood out of the wheelchair at the

Escalade. She seemingly was catching her breath, squinting from the bright Atlanta morning.

She said, "Fuck dying."

The two women kissed and separated.

PART THREE

Sexual Healing

CHAPTER 12

Keeping to her vow, Dolorian kept in touch with her friends and was disturbed to find they were doing well mentally. She hated that guys were knocking the happiness out of good-looking, sweet hearted women.

That was when she came up with the idea to take the women away, to use the money her knuckle headed, lying man gave her to take her friends away. He had given her the money to help her get over him and it was enough to make three other women happy too, she thought.

Dolorian understood the role of positive self-esteem. How a female felt about herself crucially affected every part of her life: the way she functioned at work, her female relationships. The way she felt she belonged, or didn't, in her family, and how high in life she was likely to rise. When she had poor self-esteem, a woman thought *he must be right. I am all of those things. I'd better stay with him because no one else would want me.*

The first one she called was Dia.

Dia was in the process of being a strong female by diving back into her work. She was a real estate agent who had lost her hustle when Marcus came into her life. She let him have the majority of her time; he was her man after all. It was easy to dip her nose back to the grind, Atlanta was a hot spot for real estate, residential or commercial, and she had the sexy look and smarts to be a player.

She had one comeback client whoflipped houses, who wanted her to be his own private realtor, to help him do dirt and make a lot of money. She knew, though, that she'd save that card for when she was desperate for either dick or cash.

She sat at her desk and considered calling her brother. She really missed him. He now lived in Charleston, South Carolina,

Before she got her mind to center on calling him her cell rang at her desk.

"What you doing, robbing a client?"

Dia smiled. "Not right now."

At first Dia was upset at the idea of getting away. Why hadn't she thought of that? She has money. She likes the islands. Then she considered being with them might not be fun; whining brokenhearted women on a exotic beach?

"Don't think of it like that," Dolorian said. "Think of it as a free trip and fresh start when you get back."

Sakina didn't want to go. She was beginning to take comfort in curling up alone and watching comedies until she fell asleep. She didn't want to bother watching others live unless the others were on her TV screen.

But the price of the trip couldn't be beat.

Destini was easier. Even though she didn't have vacation time left, she had taken days off to deal with her depression, she reasoned, "Fuck my job. Shit. I am bored damned near to the point of madness. I am in."

The trip began with a shopping spree through Lenox Mall. Just the shopping was therapeutic for Sakina and Dia. Dolorian was enjoying the sights of her friends, all gorgeous women, try on outfits and bathing suits.

In a high-class swim suit boutique, Destini's sweet ass was out for all to see in a thong.

"My God, do y'all see the fatness?"

They laughed respectfully, quietly.

"No, you look fine," Dia said softly.

"You little liar."

Dia's mouth gaped. "Well then you look fat. That

better?"

"I do not think I can get away with this. Not with all you skinny witches with me."

"You can," Dolorian's eyes said yes with a sultry arousal. "She'll take it. My treat."

The other women wooed.

CHAPTER 13

Dolorian took her friends to St. Martin in the Caribbean, the French side of a split island, St. Maarten was the Dutch side. Although St Martin was no longer an undiscovered slice of paradise, Dolorian had them booked into an exclusive resort with a private beach.

Stepping off the plane, Dolorian announced, "It's on now! I hope y'all are ready to have fun and new experiences."

"For sure."

"Certainly."

Destini said, "I am hot, ready and willing. Island boys, watch your bananas!" while the other ladies seemed a bit weary from the trip.

"Don't y'all fret," Dolorian announced. "I am going to get you all naked and drunk before the weekend is over."

"Ah, okay..." Dia laughed.

Dolorian bought their liquor for the weekend from a duty-free shot, lots of rum and tequila for daiquiris and margaritas...and she had to get Destini her personal bottle of Remy. She rented them a roomy Cadillac and drove them into their calming weekend spot.

Dolorian had the weekend planned, with spots for freelancing, and fun and relaxation were the key elements to it all. She took them snorkeling, fishing and charter a boat for just the four of them to just cruise the islands.

The first night she had a cook come fix them dinner in their large suite and then they had drinks at the comfy family own restaurant down the road.

They enjoyed frozen drinks, except Destini, she found herself a bottle of *Remy* at a duty-free store to enjoy. The ladies finished their first night in paradise talking jive, playing cards and watching movies on cable.

It was a nice life again, Sakina thought before she closed her eyes to give into sleep.

CHAPTER 14

The first morning Dolorian gathered her girls for a morning cruise to a nearby island for a lunch-picnic at a sandy, quiet beach.

There they ate well and stayed most of the time in the water.

Sakina, though, had a bout of depression when swimming alone. In the heat of the afternoon on the second day, when she'd lost all hope and could think only of forcing her head under the surface of the ocean till she drowned herself or leaping from one of the high cliffs and smashing her body on the rocks below.

A slight touch from Dia floating by knocked Sakina back into reality. Her thougths changed instatnly. Good friends, good times, good food...what mopre could she ask for?

By nine that evening they were all gathered in the lobby of the hotel, ready for action.

Dolorian took charge. She liked running things. She ordered a steak and seafood platter for them to share, which included alligator ribs. And she ordered two bottles of Patron and a grip of sliced limes.

"Ah, I'll be having my Remy, dear, sorry.'

"Whatever, heifer. And bring her a bottle of Remy, on the rocks."

"Bottles? Girl, you know how much all that is going to cost?'

"Nope. And I do not care. I am going home broke, spending all I brought with me. So enjoy."

The alligator ribs didn't go over so well. She and Dia were the only ones willing to try them.

"Uh, no thanks," was Destini's reaction.

"Try it, it's something new."

Dia said, "I'll try it because, shit, I've had frog legs, so how bad can it be?"

Sakina said, "I didn't even know alligators had ribs."

In the quiet of them eating, Dia said, "I never knew what a good dating relationship was supposed to be like. I never knew that I had a say in what happened on a date. I just figured you sort of go along until something feels bad."

"I really don't think men know what the fuck

they doing. They talk about they want a woman to take care of them and shit, but then they cheat, go fuck any whore that says yes."

"They act that way because, as they say, there are so many women in Atlanta. They can get away with that shit because we are desperate for male attention."

"Right. It's all about us, really."

"Don't fucking say we, us. Don't throw smart, decent women into that bowl of shit."

"Whatever, Queen Latifah over there, just because you date decent women don't make you know fucking expert. You got fucked over too, that's why you lickin' your misery away."

"Don't be acting like you know my journey."

"Bitch I do."

"Journey...Who taught you that big word?"

"Suck my ass."

"You so wish."

"Miss Angry, why are you here again? To recruit new members?"

"I was invited. Not as a loser like you, though, sweetie."

They exchanged glares, until Dolorian gave her a grin. Sakina shook her head.

"Yeah, you know."

"I know what?"

"That you going to get got."

"What? Get got what?"

"I am going to have my tongue in that ass before long."

Now Sakina laughed. "Please, okay bitch. I'm strictly dickly."

"I got one."

They all laughed.

"What you gotta say now?"

"I don't want one that has been paid for and has to be strapped on."

She got an itch on her spine, the kind that entices folk into doing something adventurous, something against better judgment; like bunji jumping off a cliff or trying a new pill everybody seems to love to get high on. The thought that not only was her man gay but she might be as well, freaked out Sakina.

"So then, why you still with the motherfucker?"

The glass stopped halfway to Destini's open, gleaming lips. She cut her a glare to Sakina. No anger though. Her eyes, her look, instead were soft, almost lost. She didn't know why she loved him, was what the look said.

"Who said I am still with him?"

"Aren't you?"

"No, officer, I am not."

Dolorian placed a hand on her arm apologetically. "My bad."

"We often don't know some fundamental truths about loved ones unless he chooses to spill the beans, or more likely, he slips up."

"Me, I think some men aren't totally honest with females when they are dating is because they're afraid they won't be liked anymore."

"That's about some baby mommas or criminal record, not the shit we got fucked with."

"But still, it goes to what I am saying. They want you but don't want to lose you before they got you."

"They end up losing you anyway in the back end, so what the fuck? Just be honest."

"There are always signs afterwards," Dia said quietly.

"True, true." Dolorian nodded.

Sakina shook her head, and said, "Like the sign that he could kill you."

There was an immense silence. That was food for thought indeed.

"Shit, that's my song!" Destini stood up and got them wide hips in motion, popping her feet out and winding her arms in unison with those hips and legs.

"Jagged Edge? Please, for real?"

"What. I love this song and fuck y'all, for real."

"She done had enough."

"I ain't get none yet."

She made them all laugh.

"I wouldn't let none of them punks suck my pussy."

"Oh, I'd let just about any fool do that."

"Really?"

"Well, look, why not? Looks ain't got nothing to do with head. I mean, that's all you gonna see is the fool's head."

She had her friends cracking up.

She was on her fourth shot of tequila.

Destini was still drinking her Remy, nice and slow, sipping it. Easy. Easy does it. Still, her head was getting light and she was feeling nice.

A group of young Black men came into the bar quietly. They added color and a sweet male scenery to the bar. The men were led to a booth. All five were a different shade of chocolate and they looked like money relaxing, with casual yet expensive island wear.

Dolorian, wildly and amazingly, immediatly thought she might want to suck a dick while in the Caribbean.

"No, uh uh. Ain't no getting my groove back shit. This is straight up horny," she shrugged. "I just want a dick in my mouth...and?"

"My God," Destini squirmed, "Miss Nasty over there."

"Shut up, all of you. Damn closet freaks. Come to the light!"

Through the laughter and the coy looks she threw the guys, Destini noticed one looking at her longer than the others. She took a deep breath and told herself to have fun.

Destini coughed in laughing, "Shit, I am down for that. I'll suck a nigga to sleep. Shit, that's what we here for, fun and nuts."

Sakina laughed so hard she damn near choked on her drink.

"I am down," Dolorian said, and all eeys came her way. "What? I like men, they well may have put a little gray in my hair but I keep coming back for more so they must have something."

"Yes, Lord. And when it is thick and has staying power, um, heaven."

Dolorian had to high-five her for that one. And the ladies drew attention with their roaring laughter.

"Well, I am looking for a man. I have run out of batteries."

"I just need me a man with some verbal skills."

"Me, I'm looking for someone that is willing to take the time to get to know me inside and then out and still be able to say 'wow'. I still like you."

"Wake up."

"Shit. I am just happy that I still want a man in my life."

"And?"

"And nothing. I had a lot of hate for men for a

minute there."

"And you were going to try the rainbow?"

"No. I ain't got to go there when I leave men alone. I got myself to make me happy."

"Been there, done that," Destini chimed. "That gets tired."

She looked and caught her admirer staring again.

One of the dudes just stared at Destini. But his eyes spoke in high volumes. She had a bra on; still her nipples were strongly evident, as if it were that time of the month. But the looker's eyes were at her eyes.

"Y'all, he likes some me," she said hiding her lips in her glass.

"Well, your girls done got you attention. You happy?"

"Huh?"

"You always are trying to make them B's into C's and now somebody staring at them."

"And? You jealous?"

"No. He can suck them. I'll get my chance."

"Ah. You wish."

"And wishes can come true."

"I am going to leave you alone before you wreck my high over here."

"I am looking for a little romance. And a lot of whatever else they bringing."

"Shut up. You are turning into a mess."

"I already been a mess. I am ready to try something new now."

Dolorian licked her lips, her eyes planted at the same spots in Destini's blouse the guy had stared at.

Destini said "It's all about the fun."

"Yes, it is."

"I need to have some serious fun. See how wet I can get."

"And what if they drug dealers?"

"Well, to find a prince these days you've got to kiss a few felons."

"Well, shit, I am sick of men and shit I might have to get licked in a minute if I can't handle my frustrations."

"Whoa."

"I gave that fucking asshole freedom for real. All he had to do was be with me. I was into that man sharing full tilt."

"What? You talking crazy. Man sharing, please now, okay?"

"Well, shit, I don't have time or energy to chase after people and beg for this and that. We respected each other's privacy and had good times together. He was very good to me when he was with me. And that was really all I wanted.

"Little did I know he was a fucking maniac. A

jealous maniac."

"I thought we were going to leave Atlanta in Georgia."

"Fuck leaving shit behind. I am still bitter, sorry."

Finally, one of the guys approached, the right one, too. He was the tallest, sexiest with his easy smile and broad shoulders.

"What's up, ladies?" His voice flowed with confidence; and the women liked it. "My name is Delvin."

They ladies cited their names.

"Well, Delvin. At least one of you have balls," Dolorian said.

"Really. We all do."

"You came to buy or cry?" Destini added.

"We're just looking for new friends. Can we join y'all?"

Dolorian looked over her friends quickly for objections and said, "Sure."

When the guy turned to get his friends, Destini whispered, "Um, Zegna. Damn he smells good."

"Oh, that's what that fragrance is? Nice."

"I hope they ain't broke," Destini said.

"I hope they ain't little dickers," Dia giggled.

The conversations were subtle. They talked about where they from, their jobs, nothing major. And it seemed, all the eyes were filled with desire and a bit of lust.

Delvin played it smartly, he captured the petite sexy ones attention then got her away from the crowd.

"Let's take a walk?" Delvin suggested.

Maurice was rather homely, with a bush of hair and none on his face. But he was lively and vibrant.

Maurice hugged her against her side. "I think I love her."

"I am temporarily wifeless."

Dolorian was watching Destini quietly. Despite the good-looking men, Destini was who she was hoping to be in bed with that night.

"Listen fellas," Dolorian said. "We are here to be with each other, so excuse us."

"Lesbos."

"That's right. So beat it before you get an asswhipping to talk about with wifey."

"I thought you wanted some dick?"

"I am picky, sorry. If you want to hang with them you are to be you."

Destini saw the want in her friend's eyes and decided to hang with her. "Naw, I wanted to but I am not in a silly mood."

CHAPTER 15

Sakina gave the guy that approached her a hard time. He wasn't bad looking, and neither was his rap; she just wasn't feeling like being picked up.

She did feel a stirring down below her gut.

Later, as she sat on a bench on the side of the hotel, facing the darkened ocean, and letting the night cool the sweat from her face, she wondered if she'd ever have another husband.

She had no memory of her husband's kiss.

She couldn't feel bad for long, not on an island and a cool breeze, thousands of miles away from her troubles.

On the real, she wanted the love of a woman. The kind of genuine, gentle caring she had experienced from Dolorian.

Even with her sour disposition she couldn't scare the guy away. The brush offs didn't work, he'd stay communicating, undeterred. And she sort of like that about him. A confident, masculine man that was into her…that felt nice.

Charles used his strong gift of gab to get her relaxed. Then he asked her to grab a table of their own.

"You don't want to sit here with everybody else?"

"No. I want to be alone with you."

"I don't know about that. It ain't that type of party here for me."

"Well, at least let me converse with you in a spot where I can hear you better."

"No see, that was smooth."

He watched Sakina's face ease as a hint of a smile curved her lips. That smile warmed him and let him know he was just about where he wanted to be, in her attention.

She got up and he rose with her as he searched for the perfect spot. She followed him to a table at the edge of the bar, facing the water.

"Oh, you know I didn't realize the bar was on a cliff."

"Scary? We don't have to sit here."

"No, this is cool."

"Yeah, it is. Isn't that water nice?"

"No, that's what's scary over here."

"Scary?"

"So dark. Like a killer waiting for a fool to come its way."

"No, no. It's calm, serene. Chilling. It's awaiting the kids, the boats, and the sea life, to all wake up, to come back and play. It's waiting on another day."

She had to smile. "Nice."

"What do you mean? That's just how I see it."

"It was poetic."

"Well, hey, I don't know about all that."

Sakina leaned on the banister. She looked down at the sand. She was picking her next words, searching for a way to tell this guy wasn't nothing sexual going to happen.

"Look, you seem cool, and maybe we can hang back in the real world, but tonight I ain't feeling what our friends are."

"What they feeling?"

She looked in his eyes. "I don't know. But we can talk, and that's it."

"That's it?"

"I didn't come down here for that."

"You want me to leave you alone?"

"No. But I don't want to waste your time, either. I am sure there is some ass out there you can get."

"Yeah. There's plenty of ass here but you know,

I am talking to you and I like it. You might be more than some ass."

She shook her head.

"Do you want to talk?"

"I moved over here with you, didn't I?"

"True that."

She sat up in the high back wooden chair and tossed her ankle over her knee. "What would you like to talk about?"

"Let's start with you."

"Me?"

"Yeah. Tell me about you."

She shook her head. *What is he up to?* She wanted to talk, though. Maybe it was the tequila. Maybe it was his calm, confident presence. Maybe her taste for a man was returning.

Delvin caught her looking and grinned. "What?"

Her blush lingered. "I was just...wondering about you."

"Yeah? Like what?"

She shrugged. "I don't want to pry."

"No, it's okay. That's what we trying to do, right? Get to know each other, right?"

She nodded.

"Well, what do you want to know?

"Are you married?"

"Not anymore."

"What did you do to her?"

"Do to her?"

"Okay, sorry. Let me put that better. My bitterness showing, huh?"

"Ah, yeah."

"Why did y'all breakup?"

He grew serious, fondling his empty glass, staring at the floor.

"Is the answer down there?"

"No, just pretty feet."

"Thank you," she said but she pushed her toes out of sight, under the table.

"Well, to be honest..."

"Yes, do that. At least start that way."

He chuckled. "That winter I was busy. Responsibilities fell heavy on me at the office."

Sakina was shaking her head.

Delvin shook his head. He said, "We were headed for a breakup. I just pushed it by not being there."

"You cheated on her?"

"Yes."

She looked away.

He could almost see the thoughts scrambling through her mind. She was apprehensive, afraid...It was the fear that ate at him.

"Now you."

"Me? I don't know. I can't tell you about who I

am now, I got hurt in my heart, but I am a laid back kind of female for the most part. I love to have fun and chill. I like movies, all kinds. I can cook and whatever the woman is supposed to do but believe me," she threw a palm up to his face, I'm no fool with mine...so don't try and run game because I have been there and done that."

"You got it."

"Um hmm."

"You going to tell me about the hurt?"

"No."

"Okay. That's cool."

CHAPTER 16

A crack of lightning illuminated the sky and a sudden breeze ran a chill through Dia and the young man that had her walking along the shoreline.

Dia folded her arms across her chest for warmth. "I thought paradise was hot," she said.

"Sometimes it rains even in paradise.

"Looks like it's going to storm."

"And that's good for indoor activities."

"Ain't none of that."

"What? I meant like board games or X Box. Or even a movie."

"That's not what you meant."

"You don't know what I meant."

She nodded.

"Okay, moving on, tell me about some of the things you like to do. And don't mention the bedroom."

Dia smiled, "I like to shop. With my man's money."

"For him?"

He wasn't intimidated and she liked that.

"Never that," she said. "That's what his girlfriend's money is for."

"Oh, really now? Well, shit, I'd like to see a honey spend money."

"You have to be my man to see me do things."

"Shit, where the applications at? I have been looking for a new woman."

"Naw, on the real though, what kind of a guy you looking for?"

"She gave him a good long stare.

"What?"

"I tell you and that will be who you become...for awhile?"

"No. I am me. Just curious about what you like in a guy."

She went on to answer because her mind was thick on the question.

"I guess what I am looking for is a decent human being. Just a regular Joe who likes to laugh and not take himself, me, or the world too seriously."

He was nodding while she spoke. Then he asked, "You want babies? You have any?"

She was so glad he asked. Most men feared ready made families as well as woman ready to make a family.

She said, "No, I am far from ready to have me some babies. Although I do want some. I love my family, including my nieces and nephews. I want me a couple.

"Do you have any kids?"

"Me? Yes. I have a daughter."

"Really? Why are you not with her mother?"

"It wasn't meant to be."

"Did you cheat one her?"

"Why you ask me that?"

She shook her head, a little embarrassed to be assuming he might have been the one.

"Well, yeah, I did cheat on her. Should have left her but I just thought things might get better."

His warmth and tenderness got her open. It was what she needed from a man right then.

She blinked her big eyes at him.

"Why are you single? Or are you?"

Dia laughed. "I am available because my man didn't like the fact that other men thought I was attractive."

"Oh, you had a jealous one."

"Yes, sir."

"Sorry about that. But I could understand."

She caught his eyes looking right in his; she had expected to bust him looking at her ass or breasts.

He whispered, "Damn you're fine."

"Thanks."

He went for a kiss and she didn't stop him. She groaned, kissing him back eagerly, pushing her tongue at him, which he greedily took. As his tongue penetrated her mouth, she felt herself melting inside.

She pressed herself against him, holding back the urgent feeling that made her want to beg for his cock. She wanted to give him herself, to experience more than a fast fuck.

She shifted her feet with a grimace.

"I bet your arches ache?"

She couldn't say no. Her feet were killing her. The strappy heels looked nice, caught this fool's eye, yet they weren't made for comfort.

"I don't know why I wore these heels."

"Because they are sexy and highlight those sexy feet and ankles."

"Got a foot fetish?"

"No. I just like yours."

The air between them warmed with intimacy. With her leg high like that, cool air reached her thong. She felt...exposed.

Her reached down and took her foot to his thigh, incredibly close to his zipper. She could shift her foot just a little bit and touch him there.

All he had to do was duck to see the place between her legs. The thought made her damp and she squirmed a bit on the chair.

His hands were talented; firm and gentle. The looser her feet and calves got, the tighter her sex became. And it was beginning to throb.

She moaned as if in pain.

He was a sexy man and right then she knew he was going to get some. But he'd have to ask right.

"What you want, baby?"

Her face was wrinkled into a bitter expression. She began to shake her head. She was drunk, she told herself, and horny as hell. She had to fight the feeling and not give this man some pussy after just meeting him.

"I can't," she said. "I don't wanna do...do anything."

"Then don't do anything. Just sit back. I am going to keep making you feel good."

Dia sighed. "We need to stop. We out in public like this."

As soon as the words came out she knew what the man would say and he said it on cue.

"Let's go back to my room."

She looked at him, eye to eye.

"Just to be alone," he answered her probing eyes. "You are in charge."

"I just met you. How would that be right?"

"Right, wrong, whatever. I just want to make love to you."

"And I don't want you to touch me like that anymore."

He didn't surrender her foot and she didn't pull away.

"We just going to talk, if that is all I want to do, right?"

"Whatever you want, but know that I want you."

They walked out and into the light rain. The winds had picked up and the storm was coming. This was his opportunity. He went for it.

"We should go inside. Want to come to my place and talk some more?"

She shook her head, "No, I think I should just go on back to my room."

Delvin took her hand. "No, come on and hang out. I promise you a good time, with nothing going on you don't want to."

His eyes had her, not his words as he thought. She nodded and he held her hand until they got to his door. As soon as he closed the door behind them, his lips found hers and no resistance. They kissed as her arms wrapped around his neck. He held the back of her neck as he placed feathery kisses on her eyes, her cheeks, her ears. *God*, she thought, *he's a really good kisser.*

"Come lie down on the couch, let me give you a full massage."

He went into his room and came out with baby oil.

"You just happened to have baby oil?"

"Well, it ain't mine. My man Dennard is dark and afraid to look ashy."

She nodded.

"You are going to take off your clothes?"

She was apprehensive. But the thought that he might put that talented tongue in her sex was too inviting.

She undressed slowly; appreciated his glowing eyes.

"Wow. You body is better than I expected."

He laid a towel on the couch to hold the lotion and give her comfort.

She slithered onto the couch and towel, on her belly, feeling both sexy and horny.

His hands went to work, at first just massaging the non-private parts. Then he stopped and he began sucking her ankles.

"No. Just massage."

He gave the ankles one more kiss, then he said, "You know what I'd like to do?" he murmured, a sinfully sexy smile easing across his too-gorgeous face. "This resort has some fly ass bathrooms. The one we got has a huge double shower. I'd like you to get in there with me, get all wet and soapy and let me make love to you like that."

She shook her head ever so slowly and smiled.

"You down?"

She had no plans to say no.

Delvin stripped off his clothes and Dia admired his thick yet firm body. He had a muscular torso tanned the color of a caramel. She had never seen a penis at rest that was as long as Delvin's.

"You're not going to be upset if you get your hair wet, are you?"

"No."

They both went into the bathroom. As she stood, surrounded by mirrors and bright lights, Delvin just looked. "You're sexy as fuck, you know that?"

"Umm."

Delvin soaped the cloth, then said, "Turn around."

She turned her back to him, and he slowly stroked her curvy rear with the soapy cloth. As she braced her palms on the tile, he rubbed down from her shoulders to buttocks, then up again.

The only sound between them was the thunder and the lightening was flashes of light that Dia felt through closed eyes.

He knelt, then soaped the backs of her thighs slowly sliding toward the insides, rubbing the slick cloth just to the edges of her pussy lips, then back to her knees. He soaped her cheeks again, then stroked between them, rubbing her anus, making her knees buckle.

"Turn around."

She almost didn't hear him. Her mind was screaming for a finger to enter her, anywhere.

She opened her eyes and saw he was hard now.

Delvin moved her under the water and she dropped her head back to wet her hair. He soaped her belly and chest, paying particular attention to her breasts, Dropping the cloth, he soaped his hands, lifted her breasts and cupped them in his hands. Water streaming them cleaned them as he continued to soap them.

A thirst was building in his throat. And although he knew he was taking a chance, he said fuck it and bowed his head. He licked the tips of her nipples and they froze in front of his eyes. Then he took the entire areola in his mouth.

Her eyes narrowed. She held the sides of his face.

That was when he knew for sure she wanted to be sexed.

They got out the shower.

Delvin rubbed her breasts lightly and continued long after they were dry. "These are beautiful."

"Thank you. You are paying them very much attention."

"There isn't anything, any part of this body I don't want to pay attention to."

Suddenly, Dia dropped the towel, put her arms under Delvin's and leaned against his whole body.

She groaned while kissing him.

He took her hand to his manhood.

She panted. Her hand was limp in his as if she was afraid to take hold of his penis.

"Just hold it for me, just touch it."

"My God," she sighed. "Oh my God."

"You like it?"

She looked up at him, "It's throbbing in my hands."

"Your hands are soft, I like that."

"You are getting hard."

"It wants you."

She was thinking about it, should she suck this man's beautiful penis? She just met him. And she wanted too. Before she could decide she was going for it, her hunger stronger than her heart and mind. She licked her lips wet and then opened her hand ran her tongue along his penis, wetting the shaft.

"Ahh," Delvin sighed. "Yes, baby."

She rose up and let her head drop over his penis, taking in as much as she could.

"Ah shit. Damn."

A desire to please him took over and she gently

sucked him and her hands tightened as she pulled back. He wasn't going to last long, and she was hell bent on taking his seed. Working her mouth in a milking suction, she claimed his sperm with choked gurgles of happiness, her tongue and fingers urging the pole to yield its full load.

Delvin was fighting to catch his breath. "That was good right there."

He led her to his bed. "Lay down."

She did.

The force of passion coming from her thick body made the rest of it easy. Didn't worry about how to please her; knew intuintaively what her body wanted, could smell it coming from her.

Her nipple stiffened in his mouth. He tugged it, rolled it between his teeth. She moaned and her legs parted. That's how simple it was.

He knew she would be wet between her legs. His fingers slid into her snug pussy, and her whole body responded. An invisible wave of arousal rolled over her that Delvin could feel in the pressure of her kiss.

He kissed his way down her chest, stopping at her nipples, then down her ribs, down the expanse of her belly. Following the coiled trail of hairs that led to the world between her legs. I wanted my mouth all over her down there. It was what she had dreamed of, ached for, she was offering it to me, wide open and juicy.

He concentrated on her neck and chest, teasing her breasts so that her nipples actually ached to be touched.

He dropped his strong hand between her legs and his big fingers pinched at her clothing, feeling her pussy. She was soaking and aching, it had been along time and this guy was getting her nice.

"I gotta eat you."

She pushed at his chest to back away and catch her breath. She said, "Is that why you and your friends came down to the island?"

"Yes ma'am. To eat American pussy, in an exotic location."

She giggled.

He fell in love with Dia's little high-hanging tits and her hint of a belly.

"Damn, baby."

And when his tongue went into her it was over. It was patient, thick and firm. And he got better. He moved his tongue up and let his fingers do the work.

With three of his fingers twirling in her, and she was very wet, he looked up for her eyes and said, "I want some of this."

"You can. Not without a condom."

Moving away from her warmth hurt his soul. He dug in his travel bag and took out a set of condoms. He was hoping to use the whole six-pack that night. He got back on the bed and the sight of her body caused him to pause. Shit, she was so fine. He placed his latex-covered cock at the entrance of her sex. Slowly he pushed.

Dia's nipples tightened, her pussy swelled and she trembled. She felt so full, so hot. She tried to keep her knees from buckling.

She was going to fuck him good and keep him around for awhile. She was going to make him her man. And this was before he put his dick in her.

She shifted her position so that she was on top, kissing and licking the fresh-sweet flesh of his chest. He moaned in satisfaction as she moved down his body.

She took the base of his swollen shaft in one hand, she used her other palm to massage his glands with a slow circular motion. They felt good in her hands and, bending her head she took first one and then another into her warm mouth, licking them until they were thoroughly wet.

His labored breathing let Dia know he was ready for the serious foreplay. Holding the base of his stiff pole in one hand, she put her lips over the head. She kept the tip of her tongue mainly over his shaft as she swallowed him, then she slowly pulled back, feeling his cock lengthen as she withdrew.

He let out a groan.

His enjoyment excited her animal passions. She was as turned on as he was. She maintained a firm, steady rhythm, making low humming sounds that caused her mouth to vibrate on his cock. His hips arched upward to meet her hungry lips.

Suddenly his hand was pushing on her head.

"Hold up. You gonna make me a short timer.

"I don't care," she faintly whispered. "I want you to cum in my mouth."

"Shit," he sighed.

She pushed him back down and took all he had into her mouth, and she forced herself to relax, swallowing as much of him as she could. He stiffened and, took her head between his hands. He spurted warm and deep into her eager mouth. She swallowed as much as she could until it was all gone.

She glanced and found he was in a dreamlike state with his eyes closed and his face flushed.

"You gotta make me hard again. I gotta get up in you."

"Yeah, you do."

She took him in her mouth again and his body responded quickly.

He moved on top of her parting her legs. The queen sized bed creaked and swayed with the violence of his thrusts.

"Easy," she whispered.

He pushed up to face her, "This shit's so good, so tight."

Her protests were useless babblings as Delvin continued his relentless grind up into her shocked pussy.

Then the pain faded away gradually until a wonderful feeling began washing over her like a rippling wave. Her first-conquered outer pussy had grown accustomed to the unusual size of Delvin's penis, and her full aroused labia were squeezing wildly, uncontrollably, around the thick wet prick that was pumping between them.

She moaned throatily as a lovely sense of pleasure echoed along the plunging path of his cock. She gave in to the passion as her entire body joyously realized the total fucking she was receiving. She closed her eyes and arched her hips to give him all he wanted. She felt him stiffen and even with the condom she felt him spurting. She tightened her ass and she dug her nails in the mattress as his throbbing triggered her own mind-blowing climax.

As spasms continued to crash over her body she felt Delvin's cock twitch, then throb as he came. All too soon his deflated penis slipped from her body.

CHAPTER 17

The man that had been staring at Destini now was up close on her, and still staring. This time he was all in her eyes.

Maurice was his name, and he was the darkest and shortest of his crew. He was also the loser, every crew has one. He was the kind of guy that got some only when it fell off a tree or the pussy was handed to him by one of his boys.

"You are so fine," was how he started at Destini.

"Am I?"

"Hell yeah you are. Big, soft and sexy."

"And how do you know I am soft?"

"I can tell?"

"Really? Well, when I first meet a man I need to check his background. See if somebody is married."

"And so what if I am married? We here on the

island to have fun and live a little."

"Really? So you just trying to fuck me tonight and that's it?"

"Something like that. But you making it sound crooked."

"Bye." She pulled away and noticed his bulge. "Nice. You happy to see me?

"Hold up?" he begged.

"There's other fish in the sea. Reload and cast away."

She thought she was walking away steady after delivering a killer line to a loser. But she was swaying off course and bumped into the corner wall and then the door as she left the bar.

She was laughing at leaving a guy hard and aching. Fuck him, was her thought, when she came upon Dolorian and one of the guys in the lobby of the hotel.

"Where you going?" Dolorian asked sternly.

"Just walking. That guy trying to turn stalker."

"Come with me."

"Ah. For what?"

"Come on." Dolorian took her hand and pulled her close. Dolorian leaned against her with her whole body.

The startled look in Destini's eyes, a mixture of fear and curiosity, turned Dolorian on.

A thirst was burning in Dolorian's throat.

"Dee, now, you need to stop. I ain't one of them girls."

"I know what you are. You are a woman I am trying to fuck."

Destini sobered. She tried to gather herself and for the first time realized she was a bit unsteady. Her eyes were wide as she scanned the lobby to see who had witnessed her turn lesbo.

She looked at the guy and he was smiling.

Dolorian was also smiling. "Come to the room, baby."

"Dolorian? I am just choice prime tonight, huh? First dude and now you all in my space."

"Fuck him."

Destini blushed.

Once in the room Dolorian sat on the couch after gathering some blunts and a bag of weed the size of a mini van. She began gutting the cigars with a pocket knife.

Destini shook her head, "Are you trying to get me fucked up?"

"And fucked. So just chill and have fun. Dolorian patted a cushion next to her. "Come join me on the couch."

"You lead I will follow," Destini giggled. "I'll try anything once."

"I like eating choice prime. It's tender."

Dolorian kissed Destini as she had never been kissed beforevery deeply, exploring her lips, her tongue, all the heights and hollows of her mouth without neglecting any spotall the while in slow motion.

Before Destini had time to realize clearly what was happening, Dolorian's hand had slipped under her shirt and in her pants, and was already taking possession of her moist sex.

"Stop."

Dolorian released her prey. She moved away, toward her room down the hall. "Come on."

"Dolorian?"

Dolorian put her key in the lock. She looked back with a sly grin before disappearing. Destini followed.

Once Destini was in she closed the door and locked in.

"I don't know," Destini said.

Dolorian shook her head. "You better know before we get started because once we do I ain't stopping until you cum in my mouth."

"Oh," she sighed softly

Then Dolorian stood up. She kicked off her shoes, unbuckled the belt of her shorts and stepped out of them, naked; the muscles tensing along her brown thighs. She got on the couch, planted one leg on either side of Destini's thick hips. She leaned down, kissed Destini's lips, then the breasts, sucking each nipple with passions. Destini stirred slightly, sighed, opened her eyes, smiled, and closed them again. Dee's mouth moved slowly downward, kissing the flat stomach, the navel, finally.

Destini moaned softly and mouthed with the half-formed expression of a woman in a dream.

Dolorian bowed her head into Destini's lap. She pushed her thighs farther apart, while her two hands widened the delicate opening. Her long tongue leapt out, and then she covered Destini's lovebox and began licking and sucking feverishly.

Dolorian, kissed, licked and sucked at the thick honey's pussy until all the thick one could do was drop her head back and moan, and then her legs began to vibrate from the thighs to the toes.

"Oh, God," Destini whined. "I never knew how good it could be."

"It's just sex, baby, just sex. And sex should always be good. Get on top."

She did. She wanted it a lot of ways that night. She stood up over her on the couch and lowered down onto the strapped on penis.

"Damn you so wet."

"It feels good?"

"Fuck yeah."

"Ride, baby."

Destini began to respond to the rubber cock poking into her. Dolorian was clinching her hips, and watching her friend cum.

"Get up," she finally said.

"Oh, so good."

"Get on your knees."

Mindlessly, she dropped to the floor and braced herself on the sofa.

Dolorian went into her room and got her bottle of lubricant. She put the bottle down by Destini's knee and admired the round ass high in front of her.

"Nice," Dolorian said.

Destini cooed. She felt a finger teasing her anus. It took her a moment to realize she liked it.

She turned her head to see who it was and her mouth was met by Dolorian's.

Destini broke off the kiss and asked, "What are you doing to my ass?"

"Loving it."

"I've never been fucked there," Destini admitted in a nearly breathless voice. "I never had the nerve to try."

Dolorian bent to give her friend some prepping. She forced her face into the back of her hips, Destini jumped at the feel of a tongue getting into her from that position. She became unsteady; it tickled, it felt good and she was about to cum again. When she did, Dolorian pulled her tongue out and licked the rim of her ass.

"You going to give this to me?"

"Yes," Destini panted, and she tensed and had to close her eyes when that talented tongue touched her hole.

Dolorian poured a generous amount of the lube over Destini's ass and cheeks.

"I like that," Destini whispered. "Feels cool"

"Relax," Dolorian whispered to Destini. "Don't fight me."

"Ah!"

The head of the strap on stretched Destini's ass to the limit, but it yielded, opening far enough to admit it.

Destini almost screamed but Dolorian caught her attention by pulling on her frozen nipples, making them burn and tingle.

"Ah! Oh!" Destini gasped. "It's not so bad. It's not so bad."

Dolorian rocked back and forth, taking in the sight. She had to touch her friend, feel her warmth. Her hands were rubbing her ass cheeks and her skin goose-bumped.

There was no longer any pain, just pressure, and her mind was on the eroticism of what was being done to her. She could feel hair on her ass and knew she had taken all of a cock in her.

Sensations of ecstasy tore through her from the feel of two hard men sliding in and out of her body. Before she could savor the moment, she felt her thighs vibrate again and lost all train of thought. She began to cum.

Dolorian came closer.

She pinched Destini's thick nipples and told her girl to ride them.

The sensations were so intense she could barely breathe. She collapsed ahead onto the sofa's cushions. Dolorian slapped her ass one more time and hard.

They rested for awhile. As they calmed their bodies cooled, enjoying a cool breeze flagging the curtains as it came through the windows.

Destini was still lit. "God, I am still hot."

"For real?"

Destini nodded.

Dolorian whirled her head around and planted a kiss on Destini's mouth, with lots of tongue involved. Then Dolorian pushed her onto her back and got her into a sixty-nine position.

"Here, eat some pussy."

And Destini hungrily attacked.

Sakina came into the suite with a whoosh of cool air

and found Dolorian above Destini's body on the floor.

Dolorian's smooth, rounded ass was bent high in the air and opened, and all her glory was showing. When she saw Destini's tongue going in, Sakina froze in shock.

"Oh."

Both women looked at her, Destini a bit embarrassed and Dolorian turned to face her old roommate, smiling.

"What in the hell?"

"It's called sex with a friend," Dolorain said with a smile, "honey, you should try it sometime.

She went in closer. "I'll just go to my room, thank you."

"No. Come join us."

"No, it's okay. You two have fun."

Dolorian went back to work and Destini silently thanked God she didn't hesitate.

Dolorian reached around her thighs, lifted them, then pressed from under her butt, pushing forward the opened center up to her mouth and feasted.

"God, you always wanted to eat me," Destini panted. "...I knew it...you wanted me." Suddenly Destini began to cum, and with such intensity, such utter abandon, she was no longer the person she knew. She moaned, shrieked, wept, and shouted fragments of curses and love.

Much later, drifting off to sleep on the sofa of the suite, Sakina remembered what tomorrow was: her wedding anniversary.

CHAPTER 18

In the morning, just before first light, Sakina left out the house to take a morning walk on the beach. Although she had only gotten a couple of hours of sleep, she felt wide awake. It was supposed to be a jog, she just didn't feel like moving faster than a stroll.

A morning in paradise was just like television depicted it, cool, warm, and breezy with great sites. The sun had ridden up over the eastern ridge. The heat was coming on faster than it had during the first two days, the mist burning off sooner.

She stopped in the sand, her sandals in her hands and took in the sights of the moderate waves crashing before they reached her feet in calm trinkles of water. Out there it seemed like there was no world out beyond the waters, just clouds and ocean forever.

It would have been six years today. Six years of marriage. A nice number, she thought. Not many of the couples she knew had made it beyond five; and now she was a part of the young and divorced.

A hunger pang made her think of the other ladies and whether they were up or not. She forced herself to think of breakfast, and then she planned out her day, things she might want to do, even though all she could think of was swimming in that clear blue-green water.

But her wedding day stole her mind. She saw him, tall and handsome, in his tux, his family all smiles, his groom's men handsome and supportive...shit, how many of them had he slept with? Asshole.

Wallace was coming to her, the Reverend offered her to be kissed, and Wallace kissed Sakina as if he loved her.

She could see it. The DVD. Him holding her in a tight embrace. His lips crushing hers and his tongue going in her mouth.

She could see it, recall the moment, but she could not feel it anymore.

The sounds of male voices awoke Dia.

She was having another deep, yet dreamless, sleep and the chatter frightened her awake.

A man came to the bed, smiling, and for a solid second she could not recognize him.

"Good morning," the good-looking guy said. "Have breakfast with us?"

She remembered; but not his name. Damn.

"No thanks."

Dia twirled out of the bed and was naked.

"Wow, you look good."

She was looking around the room.

"Your clothes are right there. Would you like to shower?"

She moved to them and dressed. The guy sobered.

"Hey, what's up?" he said softly. "You all right?"

"I didn't sleep well," she began but decided to not whine. "I am not a morning person."

"Well, just come on, chill out. We making breakfast, you can lay down until its ready then I can walk you back to your room."

She smiled at his kindness. "That's good, I am glad you asked me but I just rather go now."

"Okay. I'll see you later?"

"I don't know."

"You don't know?"

"You caught me vulnerable."

"Wait a minute...Hold the fuck up, ain't nobody take advantage of you."

She slapped a palm to her head. She was dressed except for her shoes. "I didn't say that. I am just not emotionally available. I shouldn't have done

175

anything with you last night."

The dude sighed. "Well, forget...let's not lose a chance at friendship is what I am trying to say."

She was ready to go.

"Can I see you later?"

"If you want to, sure.

"Of course I want to see you, don't play."

"Eight oh four. That's my room."

"Eight oh four. Got it."

When she got back to their suite, the place was quiet. So quiet she could hear the water running in the back. She got to her bedroom and stripped naked and lay across the bed until she could shower off and the start the day new.

She lay there on her belly, a pillow squeezed in one arm, trying not to think; not to think about the sex from the night before and of course that image came to her vividly.

Delvin was his name.

Delvin had done her right. He was good to her body. Her pussy tingled at the memory of his tongue. She closed her eyes and sleep came back at her.

Destini stepped out from the tub and toweled herself dry. She was humming softly. Her mind on a new hit tune radio was playing to death...a new upbeat Jill Scott jam.

That's how they get you, she thought, playing a song over and over until you just had to have it. Then she recalled that was Boo's attitude about radio. He only listened to CDs, his kill-a-nigga rap, no radio. "No same fucking songs every hour in my ride."

Fucking loser. Fuck him and his own fucking music.

Wouldn't he like to know I have turned to women, she thought with a smile

Wait. No. Wouldn't he like to know I am straight freaky now. Anal. A threesome, foursome! Lesbo action.

Unbelievable...that's me.

A memory of how sweet Dolorian's tongue had felt sent a chill down her spine.

She's no freak, she thought again. It was all about fun, fun and sex.

CHAPTER 19

Dolorian was the first to join Sakina on the beach.

"I was wondering where you went."

"Just enjoying the view."

"Nice."

"It's going to be hot today."

"Yes."

Dolorian settled down on the next beach chair, crossed her legs and sighed. That was when Sakina noticed her girl had a drink in her hand.

"Isn't it a little early for that?"

"No ma'am. Not at all. Shit, I already smoked one."

"What is it?"

"Margarita. Peach. Want some?"

"Let me get a sip. Just a little."

"Don't be shy."

They met eyes and smiled.

Sakina decided to ask. "What was last night about?"

Dolorian didn't move or change expression. For half a second she thought to lie but thought better of it. Why lie to her girl, her best friend?

"It was the attention. She needed it. And, perhaps, the five shots of *Patron* she drank."

"And?"

"And what?"

"I didn't know Destini swung like that."

"I ain't going there. It was what it was, that one night of sex. I think she was curious and I liked her body. Nothing more, nothing less."

Sakina was shaking her head, her eyes out across the calm sea.

"She told me that was the first time she had ever made love to a woman, and I believe that's the truth. The point is that she is all bottled up; so bottled up that she doesn't know what she feels. Apparently the only guy she had slept with was her ex, and with him she was frigid. She didn't even play with herself until I made her. So how come she did what she did with me?"

Dolorian savored the taste of the Peach margarita, letting it trickle back slowly down to soothe her throat. It tasted almost as good as Destini's pussy. For a moment she contemplated the notion of taking

Sakina up to their room and throwing a quick fuck into that sexy body, but instead she caught a dark-skinned waiter and ordered another drink.

She said to Sakina, "After another drink I'll try and think up some answers."

Sakina smiled and her mind drifted that instantly. She was back in Atlanta driving on 285 going somewhere.

Dolorian snapped her mind back to the present. "Let me ask you something. Why were you so hard on ole boy? He was kinda cute and he seemed like he wasn't talking stupid."

Sakina looked away, out to a guy on a tiny boat, drifting. She decided to be truthful. "I didn't want him at first."

"That was obvious."

"I wanted you," Sakina said. "I wanted us."

Dolorian stopped smiling. She was shocked to hear her dear friend admit a different kind of love.

"One morning in the hospital I was staring at the ceiling, and I had to admit I am a lesbian. No bi-curious, straight woman would spend so much time thinking about women, fantasizing about sex with women."

Sakina went on, "I was out there for a while. Dreaming. I would read personal ads on one of those internet sites. Women seeking women. It got really old and unfulfilling quick. I wasn't trying to meet none of them women. Just dreaming. Wallace had some X-rated movies and I'd skip to the girl-girl scene, all of them movies have at least one," she giggled.

Dolorian shook her head and smiled.

"It was quite addictive, I must say."

Again Dolorian just nodded. She was considering all of what her friend was saying, what she was really getting at.

"Now that I am single for real and fresh off suicide because of a man, I have all the freedom needed to explore my sexual identity." Sakina sighed, "One of my favorite fantasies was a ménage a trois with you and that beautiful female you used to date senior year. Dreaming about y'all! I had never felt that aroused in my life."

Dolorian frowned and smiled, *who was she talking about? And why was she fantasizing when all she had to do was ask?*

Sakina saw her unknowing eyes. "You remember, you can't forget her, she wore those jeans and sandals all the damn time. Long golden brown hair and big teeth."

Dolorian chuckled. "Big teeth. Funny. And big breasts. You're talking about Vernice."

"Yes. Vernice. Vernice. I can't believe I couldn't remember her name. I wanted you two to just do me."

"And we could have. She liked you."

"Really?"

"She knew better than to say anything."

"Wow. She liked me. Maybe I am a lesbian."

"A female finding you sexy does not make you a lesbian, Kina."

"I know that. I mean, I am not confused. I am sounding mixed up but I am not confused."

Dolorian turned to her. "Whatever," she said softly.

"Whatever?"

She took Sakina's hand and squeezed it gently. "I love you, Kina. It's whatever. I'll be in your life in whatever way you'll have me. Forever."

"I love you, Dolorian. I do."

Dolorian ached to kiss her, and she would have, long and passionately, but at the last second she saw that their friends were coming across the sand.

"It's not about the fact that you saved my life. It's not about the fact that my husband turned out to be gay. But through all of this, because of all of this, I know that I love you."

They held hands for a long moment and then let go with the silent promise to get back to their discussion at a better time.

CHAPTER 20

The other women joined them in a rush of chatter and cool air.

"Get a room!" barked. "Lezzies."

"And you liked it."

"And I did. And now, honey, back to dicks."

"Ah, what are y'all talking?"

"This here for grown folks, hussy," Destini laughed.

"And whatever. I just had me another massage. I am damn near addicted."

"To his dick or his hands?"

"No happy endings. Remember? It's never that type of party."

The other two settled in and calm overcame the four like an old friend.

"This is the fucking life."

"This is how it's supposed to be for beautiful women."

"This is how it is; we just been lost in the scuffle of living broke."

"Yeah, ain't nobody balling like you."

"Shit, you can be."

"Ah, no. The only stripping I do is to get in the shower."

"I wish we had more time."

"We don't have to leave in the morning."

"Yes, some of us do."

Delvin, shirtless in colorfully bright and baggy swim trunks, strolled up on the ladies.

Dia's body tensed at the sight of his bronzed chest and thick arms and legs.

"Hello."

"Hi," she said softly. "You remember my friends?" And she introduced them, proud to now know his name.

"Care to swim with me?" he asked.

"Sure."

He offered his hand, and after a second pause, she gave hers to him and they walked to the ocean.

"She fucked him," Destini announced. "...and well."

"Most def," Dolorian nodded.

"Yeah, well you had fun."

"Excuse you?"

"Them walls are supposed to be soundproof but I heard you right through them."

"You should have been doing something, not listening in."

"You don't know what I might have done last night."

"Please."

"I know what you might have done," Dolorian said, "but sadly you didn't do shit."

"I am a lady."

Dolorian and Destini busted into laughter.

"Anyway," Destini said. She stood, "Y'all trying to depress a bitch and shit. Ah, no thanks. I am getting in that good ass water some more before we out."

They watched her meaty hips splash into the sea. She dove in and swam the back stroke until her body had gone nearly a mile away. They eye Destini's body float in the clear blue water like a piece of drift wood.

Dia came back, almost dry from the sun and reclaimed her seat. She wasn't smiling, and hadn't been gone long enough to have enjoyed herself, but the ladies didn't pry. They could tell her mind was in motion.

Dia was thinking, did I fuck him because I was lonely? Fuck the payback he wanted. Fuck what you did to me. She shook her head. I didn't do shit to deserve what he did.

"I want to get them," Dia said out of nowhere, snapping into her friends' conversation.

Strangely, none of the ladies replied at first. It was like they all had been waiting for someone to say it and Dia was the perfect one of them.

"What you talking?" said Destini, back from her swim.

"You know what I am saying." Dia didn't return the glares. She was looking out across the clear skies, watching an image of herself kicking Marcus' ass.

"Revenge," Dolorian nodded her head and looked out into the future too. "And I feel it."

"No, no, see? Y'all are trippin'." That was Destini, and she wasn't feeling it. It was over and she didn't want to go back there, to that hurt, she was cool with never seeing Boo again. Fuck him, had been her thought.

"How we tripping?" Dolorian asked.

"Let the shit go."

Dia hesitated then swallowed. Her voice cracked. "Fuck tripping and fuck letting it go. I am with it, whatever. These fools just going to walk away from the hurt. Fuck that playboy shit."

There was a deep silence.

There they all sat, seemingly four sensual, sexy, and together women surveying paradise and thinking of vengeance.

Destini shrugged. "The Lord will take care of them," she said.

Dolorian said, "And the devil in them will not let them see the payback unless we standing right there."

"That's what I am saying." She turned to Sakina and they met eyes. "Fuck them. Let's get 'em."

Dolorian threw up her hand for a high-five. Destini gave in. "Fuck them," she said and gave her girl a high five.

"Now. Let's have some more fruity drinks, chill a bit more, have fun and all that, then let's go home and do damage to some stupid niggas back in America."

The ladies all laughed, even Dia, and they relaxed. Deep down, though, the feeling some form of revenge was about to jump off had them a little giddy and a tad bit nervous.

Their time on the island ended like it was supposed to, just the ladies sitting on the beach, in their bathing suits under umbrellas with a couple of pitchers of margaritas...and of course, Remy Martin.

They all knew once back on the mainland their lives would be the same but different. And nothing as relaxing as when they could be together.